While her husband, Sherlock Holmes, is off playing detective in London, Irene Adler finds herself having to turn investigator when her friend Renata becomes the prime suspect in the attempted murder of her husband, Luigi Amato. How can she refute the testimony of a credible eyewitness, even though her heart tells her that Renata is innocent? What she needs is tangible evidence, and she's willing to do what she must to obtain it.

When Sherlock finally arrives on the scene, Irene seeks his counsel, and he agrees to assist with her investigation. However their relationship is called into question by Irene's dear friend Sophia, who is not overly fond of Irene's husband nor approving of the way in which they conduct their marriage. Will Irene be able to prove her friend Renata's innocence, or is there a more tangled web of deception at play? And will Sophia's misgivings regarding her marriage bear unfortunate fruit?

Meet Me In Milan
Copyright © 2023 KD Sherrinford
ISBN: 978-1-4874-3968-2
Cover art by Martine Jardin

Published by eXtasy Books Inc

Look for us online at:
www.eXtasybooks.com

Meet Me In Milan
Sherlock Holmes and Irene Adler Mysteries 3

By

KD Sherrinford

DEDICATION

For my Golden girls, Jayne Leahy and Ganya Dagnall.

Acknowledgements

This book has been inspired by the works of Sir Arthur Conan Doyle, featuring characters recognizable from his original stories.

Creating my Sherlock Holmes and Irene Adler Mysteries, including this third book in the series, has been a remarkable journey, and it would not have been possible without several people's unwavering support and dedication.

I want to extend my heartfelt gratitude and acknowledge the contributions of everyone who contributed significantly to bringing this project to life.

My development editor Abigail McIntosh, thank you for sharing your unique perspectives and insightful feedback, which enriched my writing beyond measure. To Gayna Dagnall and Jayne Leahy, for your encouragement and commitment to this project, which sometimes went above and beyond the call of friendship.

To Tony and Barbara Waslin-Ashbridge, for their invaluable support and contributions.

I extend my appreciation to my wonderful friends and family, my husband John, my son David, and my daughter Katie who was instrumental in helping me breathe life into Irene Adler. Your encouragement, patience and belief in my abilities as a writer helped fuel my determination to continue with this series.

To the amazing publishing team at Extasy Books, the ever-patient EIC Jay Austin, and Martine Jardin for her fabulous covers.

Special mention to Alan Johnson and Annette Tarpley from The Passion of Poetry, Benedetta Cinquini for her invaluable help with her Italian translations. Steve Thorpe, Jon Oshiro and Elena Constanapoulou from The Sign of Holmes for their extraordinary kindness.

Lastly, I express my deepest gratitude to the readers and everyone who embarked on this incredible journey with me. I hope Sherlock and Irene's adventures continue to fire your imagination and leave an indelible mark on your memories.

PROLOGUE

Our most significant mishaps don't always involve misunderstandings. Instead, they occur when we dwell too long on our mistakes. No one gets everything right—except my husband, of course. The most celebrated detective of his time, Sherlock Holmes.

It was the summer of 1905, seven months after a Christmas reconciliation with Sherlock's brother, Mycroft, at our farm on the Sussex Downs.

A decade had passed since Sherlock Holmes burst into my life, and it had been an incredible journey. Thanks to my husband, the dark shadows of my past no longer defined me. Finally, I could look in the mirror and see a strong independent woman staring back. The memories that tormented me had now disappeared.

To the outside world, I was happily married to Lucca Sapori. To ensure the safety and protection of our beloved children, who proved that good could come out of life's darkest moments, Sherlock and I agreed that we would maintain the facade. The terms of our relationship ostensibly bound us, so we continued with our life of duplicity, secure in the knowledge that love does not diminish with age nor by distance. Time may pass and fade away, but the memories we made together will forever linger.

Chapter One: The Amatos

Shakespeare once acknowledged that words sometimes fail us, meaning that there must be moments in life when it is best to stay silent and keep our thoughts to ourselves. If only I'd followed that advice in the summer of 1905, then my life would have been far less complicated, and a simple misunderstanding would not have put me at odds with the man I adored.

Rehearsals had already begun at La Scala for Richard Wagner's opera *Das Rheingold*. Touring Europe with the production in autumn, I was excited to play Erda, Mother of the Earth, while my friend Sophia would play Fricka. Fascinated by how music brought people together, and how a particular piece can transport one back to a memory, I had been fortunate to receive considerable acclaim and encouragement in my career as a contralto.

In opera, and especially acting, the element of acceptableness for women is miniscule. I will never forget the discourteous taunts that affected me profoundly as I battled my way to the top of the misogynistic world of my profession. Over the years, I've witnessed bullying and incessant racism towards my colleagues and myself in a male-dominated world, and I have often called it out. In addition to performing, I also valued my time teaching at the theatre school—working alongside the maestros, helping to inspire and shape the next generation.

It was the end of the school term. Violetta and Ludo Espirito kindly offered to take my children, Nicco, ten years old, and Charlotte, five, on a tour of Fiesole.

Before their trip, I decided we needed quality time together, a little light relief before the children embarked on their journey. Accompanied by Sophia and her children, Gabriella and Gianni, we took a carriage into town. First we visited the Galleria Vittorio Emanuele 11 shopping mall, where I bought Nicco and Charlotte clothing for their trip. Then, as a surprise, Sophia and I took the children to Parco Sempione, a striking public grassland adjacent to the lush gardens of the Sforza castle, an historical site and museum. We spent a wonderful afternoon with a picnic of bread, cheese, ham, lemonade, sweetbreads, and fresh fruit. Sophia and I sat on a blanket, our parasols shielding us from the glare of the afternoon sun, as we watched the children run around, screaming with glee.

Due to their eclectic knowledge far beyond their tender years, Nicco and Charlotte differed from the other children. However, they never allowed their superior intellect to interfere with their relationships with others.

As I watched the children play, I remembered the last time we'd come to the park, three months ago, after we'd returned from a family holiday in Rome. We had a wonderful time in the park, exploring the museum. Afterwards, Sherlock took us to the Duomo Cathedral, the pinnacle of gothic architecture and the largest of its kind in the world, which took over 500 years to complete. These were such fond memories.

Over the years, Sherlock and I had grown to love Milan with all its diversity and culture. We adored the art, poetry, and music of the city, apart from the many great operas we attended during our time there. We were also fans of the Ambrosian Chants, the first codified music in western culture. Sherlock and I agreed with Wolfgang Amadeus Mozart's astute observation that music is not in the notes, but in the silence between.

After three months apart, the longest we had ever been away from each other, I missed my husband terribly. Even though we were both extremely busy with our careers, I still felt lonely at times. Sherlock and I kept in touch by letter or telegram. He sent me a single red rose every Monday in memory of our first meeting at La Scala.

I was thrilled to receive a letter from him a few days earlier, telling me to expect him home on Saturday. He would send a telegram to confirm his arrival later in the week, his usual custom. I could hardly wait to see him again. That incomparable feeling at the pit of your stomach, the excitement of knowing you would soon meet, those feelings remained as intense as when we'd first met.

We intended to spend a few days together in Florence, before travelling to Fiesole to meet the children and see our old friends. Ludo collected Nicco and Charlotte on Thursday morning in his new Panhard et Levassor automobile.

Charlotte stared up at me with her beautiful blue eyes, with an air of reflectiveness that Sherlock often remarked was quite extraordinary for a five-year-old. "Will Daddy be coming with you to collect us?" she asked.

I nodded. "Yes, he will. Your father is looking forward to seeing you both. First, however, I want you to be on your best behaviour for Ludo and Violetta."

"We will, mother," said Nicco. "We can't wait to see Francesco."

After hugging them, I watched Nicco and Charlotte climb into the car. Ludo checked they were correctly seated and comfortable before taking his place at the wheel. Turning to me, he said, "Don't worry, Nene. The bambini will be fine with Violetta and me."

"Thank you," I said. "Please send my regards to Violetta. Tell her I look forward to seeing her soon."

Holding back my tears, I watched the car until it rounded

the corner and faded into the distance. I then made my way into the villa, located close to La Scala, on one of the prettiest streets in Milan, Via Torino. The villa looked stunning in the sunlight, with its blue verandas, expansive ornate gardens with topiary hedges, and immaculately kept flower beds. Despite the domestic servants pottering around the house, it felt quiet and empty without the children and my husband. Yet I could feel their presence in every room. I would miss Nicco and Charlotte and the sound of their infectious laughter. Still, I was comforted knowing I would see them soon, along with their father.

Apart from my husband's insights, advice, and humour, I missed the simple things. Like the way he looked at me when I walked into a room. Sitting in front of the fire, him with his pipe and me with a cup of coffee. I even missed his cynical observations and cutting remarks, usually directed at me. The way he cast his eye over you with a cold stare or lifted you with a soft word and a smile. The eccentricities that make him the great detective that he is. Being with Sherlock taught me one thing — love and life can be complex at times. And, although I was married to a man who was sometimes more mystifying than any of the cases he solved, life became a little less convoluted with him by my side.

With the servants gone for the night, the twilight proved oddly repressive, so I was relieved when Sophia's hansom arrived later that evening. We'd been invited to dinner with our newest cast member, Renata Amato, and her husband, Luigi, who'd married earlier that year. The carriage ride under the blue abyss of the night sky was pleasant on our journey to one of Milan's most affluent areas, Centro Storico.

The coachman pulled up outside the wrought iron gates of the Amato's double-fronted detached villa, set in a four-acre compound. The lawn in front of the white-painted house with its green borders was a semi-circle of four beautiful garden beds all adorned with roses. They looked stunning, shimmering in the moonlight in colours of red, yellow, pink, and white.

A diminutive and neat maidservant answered the door and ushered us inside. We were first greeted by opulent marble archways and the splendour of a wide hallway with highly polished wooden floors and Aubusson rugs. We walked through a pair of arched doors leading into the light and well-appointed drawing room, its windows looking out onto a vibrant green oasis of pristine landscaped gardens, coral peonies, gerbera daisies, and olive groves. I lingered for a moment, taking in the picturesque scenery. Sophia and I agreed — this was a place that defied all expectations.

Observing our approach, our hosts came forward and effusively greeted us. But, in truth, I was curious to meet Luigi Amato. He was a tenor of distinguished skill and success who owned his own theatre company in the old town of Milan. I had never worked with Amato, but according to a friend of mine, he led a sedentary lifestyle and had quite a reputation with the ladies. Still, anyone was capable of change. And I was not disappointed. Luigi Amato was tall, of medium build, probably in his mid- to late-thirties, bright-eyed and handsome, clean-shaven with dark hair and an engaging manner. He was dressed in a well-cut black three-piece suit, his white shirt puckering under the strain of his lean, muscular physique.

Renata was to play Woglinde in our forthcoming production, so we had much to discuss. She was a beautiful woman in every sense of the word. She wore an exquisite black silk gown that enhanced her tall and slender figure. She had dark hair with an aquiline profile and mesmerising blue eyes. The Amatos made a handsome couple. Luigi continually peppered his wife with compliments, and I noticed a special glint in Renata's eyes when she looked at her husband.

Sophia took a sip from her glass, staring at Renata curiously. "Where did you and your husband meet?"

Renata beamed at my friend. "Luigi and I met in Genoa, where I was raised. I was training at the Teatro Carlo Felice when I first saw Luigi performing as Marcello in *La Boheme*. I was introduced to him at the after-show party, and the attraction was immediate."

Luigi shook his head, waving his hand dismissively, before addressing us. "Ladies" — he smiled widely at Sophia and me — "I was enamoured from the first time I saw Renata. I couldn't imagine anyone more beautiful. She was enchanting and I was determined to marry her. So I'm ashamed to say that I pursued her relentlessly until she finally gave in and agreed to become my wife. When she said yes, that was the happiest moment of my life."

"You old romantic." Renata stared adoringly at her husband.

"And what about you ladies?" asked Luigi. "Where are your husbands this evening?"

Sophia replied, "Well, as you know, my husband Robert is the musical director at La Scala. Unfortunately, he's currently away on a lecture tour in London. And as for Nene, her husband Lucca works in Westminster. Although we expect our husbands to return home by the weekend."

"Why, that's a shame." Renata shifted her gaze to me. "You must miss your husband terribly."

"Yes," I agreed. "I do. But Lucca and I have been together a long time. We have separate careers, so separation is something we've become used to over the years. From personal experience, finding a decent man is as rare as finding a needle in a haystack."

"Well, ladies, I shall look forward to meeting your husbands. You must all come to dinner when they return from London." Luigi took a puff of his long black cigar.

"Oh, we would love to, wouldn't we, Nene?" Sophia concealed her grin under the rim of her glass. "I'm sure Robert and Lucca will look forward to us having dinner together."

I glared at Sophia, before turning my attention to our hosts. "My husband is not a fan of social events. However, I'm sure he will make an exception in this case."

"But what does your husband do, Nene? What is his occupation?" Renata stared at me with an air of curiosity.

Sophia coughed into her napkin, desperately attempting not to laugh.

"My husband works for the British Government, I'm afraid I cannot divulge what he does. To be honest, I'm not exactly sure."

"No matter," said Luigi, before refilling our wine glasses. "Renata and I shall look forward to meeting the infamous Mr Sapori. I have already had the pleasure of meeting Signor Moon, of course. In addition to you delightful ladies, Robert and the rest of the ensemble cast have been instrumental in helping Renata settle in at La Scala. Thank you for that."

We finished dinner with coffee and brandy, leaving earlier than expected as Luigi complained that he was feeling unwell with indigestion. "Too much wine and rich food," he joked.

Sophia squeezed my hand as the driver pulled up outside my villa. "Why don't you come stay with the children and me? Gabriella and Gianni would be delighted to see you."

I shook my head and kissed my friend on the cheek. "Thank you for the offer, my dear, but I will be fine."

Sophia caught my arm as I disembarked from the carriage. "Forgive me, I had no wish to upset you. Still, you know how I feel about Holmes. You deserve so much more than he is prepared to give. Love to that man is nothing more than an abstract word."

I shook my head. "No, you are quite wrong. We have been

through this before, Sophia. I know you barely tolerate Sherlock, but he's my husband and the father of my children. And despite all his faults, he has never raised a hand to me, neither has he cheated or lied. How many wives do you know who can say that?"

Sophia looked taken aback for a moment, then she smiled whimsically. "Yes, you're right, of course. I know I am overreacting after all these years, and I'm sorry, but you know how much I care for you. Tell me, how long has it been since you and Sherlock last saw one another?"

"Ninety-nine days."

Sophia cocked her head to one side. "Ah, so you're not counting, then."

We laughed. Sophia always had a knack for cheering me up. We embraced warmly before bidding each other good night.

The coachman waited until I put my key in the lock before continuing his journey. I stepped across the threshold, shutting the door behind me. I felt the walls closing in on me like a child's embrace. I may have been alone, but I was home where my beloved children and husband would join me shortly, although I was disappointed to discover no telegram had arrived as expected.

Slipping into the drawing room, I poured a glass of wine, staring at the clock as it struck midnight. An overwhelming desire to speak to Sherlock washed over me. Although we would meet in two days, I would have sold my soul to be able to sit with him and hear his voice at that moment. I pondered if he'd already started his journey to Milan.

I guessed I would know precisely where he was if we had a normal relationship. But then our relationship was far from conventional, something that had never before bothered me. Instead, I valued the freedom our bond gave me to continue my career and spend time with my loved ones and friends.

My husband and I understood each other's need for independence.

We had agreed I would take the children back to New Jersey the next year so they could continue their education in America. Sherlock was keen for Nicco to eventually go to Harvard, and he wanted the best education possible for Charlotte, as Harvard did not admit women. I was glad that Nicco and Charlotte would receive the education they deserved, but I was concerned that my relationship with their father might come under strain. Although I knew I must follow my father's and husband's wishes and put the children first, I was confident that Sherlock and I would work things out as we had done throughout the years.

I poured another glass of wine, reflecting on what Luigi had eloquently said about his wife. I smiled to myself. I couldn't imagine my husband saying that about me, at least not in public. Sherlock was an intensely private man. Of course, he whispered words of endearment to me during our most intimate moments.

The night before he returned to London, I remembered the last thing he said as I lay in his arms. "Don't worry. I shall be back before you know it to meet you once again in Milan." Sometimes, when in a melancholy mood, I yearned for my husband to be more spontaneous, although I knew when we married that was unlikely to happen.

I opened the bureau desk and removed a cigarette case and a box of Swan vestas matches. I lit one, savouring the taste. I would hardly be described as a smoker. But now and then, when I felt agitated, apprehensive, or a little stressed, I found that nicotine alleviated the symptoms.

I looked up at the clock on the wall. It was 1 AM. I drained my glass, put the cigarette in the ashtray, and retired to bed.

CHAPTER TWO: THE POISONING ⁊

I woke up early the following morning.
Before embarking on my journey to La Scala, I showered, changed, and had a breakfast of Caffé noir and fresh fruit. It was a lovely day, so I walked to the Opera house for our final rehearsal before the summer vacation. I found Renata and Sophia waiting patiently for me in the green room.

We made our way into the auditorium to start rehearsal with the rest of the ensemble cast. A real buzz was going around the theatre that morning as our principal conductor, Leopoldo Mugnone, arrived. Originally from Naples, he was a dark-haired imposing man with a moustache and beard, of medium build, attired in a brown three-piece suit and a bow tie. We were all thrilled to be working with Mugnone. He was a conductor of exemplary reputation, said to have been held in very high esteem by the late Giuseppe Verdi.

There was collective excitement throughout the auditorium as rehearsals began. Sophia and I stared in awe as Renata performed scene one, *"Weia! Waga! Woge, du Welle,"* in her beautiful soprano voice. We all observed her breathtaking performance with gasps of admiration. This talented girl reminded me of Ava Espirito, who had burst onto the scene and taken La Scala by storm. Sophia and I smiled at each other. We knew what it felt like to finally arrive.

At the same time, Mugnone's stage direction was thrilling, innovative, and respectful of the piece and its composer, Wagner, who had found inspiration for *Das Rheingold* in a dream.

We broke from rehearsals just before three o'clock. Renata and I had just said our goodbyes to Sophia, waving as her

rriage pulled away, when a solemn-faced constable from
he Polizia approached Renata, speaking to her gravely.

"I am sorry to tell you, Signora Amato, that your husband
collapsed at home earlier this morning. The housekeeper
raised the alarm and an ambulanza was called and took him
to the Policlinico Hospital. The doctors suspected food poisoning at first, but then your husband's symptoms became
more severe, synonymous with strychnine poisoning, as the
symptoms are similar."

Renata burst into tears. 'But my husband was fine this
morning, Officer. There must be some mistake.'

"There was no mistake. We have a car outside. We can take
you to him."

Renata nodded and turned to face me. "Nene, will you
please come with me?"

"Yes, of course."

We arrived at the hospital twenty minutes later. Luigi lay
on a bed, pale and drawn, unrecognisable from the man we
had dined with the night before. Renata sat down on the chair
beside the bed, her eyes flooded with grief. The *consulente*,
Ferrari, entered the room. He was a middle-aged man with
dark receding hair, wearing a white coat with a stethoscope
around his neck.

Ferrari grimaced as he approached, addressing Renata and
the constable with a fixed stare. He sighed, then hesitated for
a moment before continuing. 'We couldn't be certain, but having dealt with similar cases, as a precautionary measure, we
administered tannic acid, which precipitates the strychnine as
an insoluble tannate salt. We have anaesthetised your husband with chloroform until the effects of the strychnine wear
off. We questioned your husband whether he had attempted
to take his own life, which he denied. He said he knew nothing of any poison, leaving us to suspect the poison had been
administered maliciously. We had no alternative but to notify

the Polizia.

"Was your husband unhappy or depressed? Do you think it is possible he may have tried to take his own life?" quizzed the constable.

Renata shook her head. "No. On the contrary, we were, in fact, very happy together. I don't understand. Luigi would never try to kill himself.

"So, are you saying Luigi could have been deliberately poisoned?" I gasped.

"It's a distinct possibility. One we cannot rule out." The constable nodded to Renata sympathetically. "We must speak to your husband once he has recovered, and carry out routine checks. You should go home now, Signora Amato. My inspector will interview you in the morning. Can you come to the station at ten o'clock? Or I can ask Inspector Romano to call at your house, if you prefer."

I nodded to the constable. "I think Renata should come home with me. I don't think she should be left alone under the circumstances." I opened my bag and quickly scribbled out my address which I handed to the constable. Then I did the same on a separate sheet of paper before passing it to Ferrari.

"You have my details. I would like you to update us on any progress in Signor Amato's condition. In the meantime, we shall expect Inspector Romano tomorrow morning. We will take our leave from you now."

The constable nodded. "Our carriage is outside. Please allow me to offer you a lift, Signora Sapori."

"That is very gracious of you, thank you."

Back at the Villa, with still no word from Sherlock, I dismissed the servants for the night. I poured out a stiff brandy for Renata and me. She sipped slowly from the glass, her hands shaking and her face as white as a sheet. I handed Renata a clean night dress and made her comfortable in the guest bedroom, sitting with her until she finally drifted off.

Slipping downstairs, I was pouring a glass of wine when I was disturbed by a knock at the door. After a few moments, my maid ushered Sophia into the room. She raised an eyebrow, observing my sombre expression.

"I'm sorry to disturb you at this late hour, but I couldn't bear the thought of you being alone." Sophia furrowed her brow. "What is it, Nene? What has that consulting detective done now?" she asked with a glimmer of sarcasm in her voice.

"Nothing, that's the problem. I expected a telegram and it never arrived, which is out of character for Sherlock. And, I'm not alone. Renata is staying with me tonight."

Sophia raised an eyebrow, staring at me curiously. "I'm sure there will be a logical explanation for Sherlock's absence. He will arrive soon, you'll see. But tell me, why is Renata here with you? Has there been some altercation with Luigi?"

I shook my head, taking Sophie's hand in mine. "Sit for a while, take wine with me, and I will tell you everything." Sophia agreed, and we sat on the chaise lounge together. I filled her in on all that had transpired at the theatre and the hospital.

"It's a good thing Sherlock is on his way. It appears Renata and Luigi will need his help." Sophia squeezed my hands, observing my subdued expression. "I can tell that, like me, you have become very fond of Renata. Why, she is like a sister. Don't worry, my dear. If anyone can get to the bottom of this bizarre affair, then it will be your husband. I shall call and check on you tomorrow. In the meantime, please do not hesitate to send for me if there is anything I can do."

After Sophia left, I retired to bed. I couldn't sleep as I lay on top of the sheets on what was a hot and sultry night, closing my eyes and wondering what Sherlock would think of the events that had transpired so far. It was inevitable that our vacation would have to be put on hold.

CHAPTER THREE: THE ACCUSATION

W e'd barely finished breakfast when Inspector Romano
and his sergeant arrived at the villa on Saturday morning. I dismissed the servants, inviting the men to take coffee
with us in the morning room. After introducing us to his sergeant, Romano took me to one side to speak to me briefly in
confidence. The inspector said he remembered me from my
adventures with Holmes in 1895. He hadn't changed much,
although he was greyer and had put on weight since our last
encounter.

His weight gain suited him. I was aware that Romano was
one of the few people who knew Sherlock and I were secretly
married, and was always on standby to offer us protection if
it were ever needed. But, as professional as ever, he never
mentioned a thing in front of Renata and his sergeant.

Romano took out his notebook and pen. "Signora Amato, I
am sorry we are meeting under such trying circumstances,
but may I ask you to relay your whereabouts yesterday?"

"I left home at eight-thirty am. Rehearsals were due to
commence at La Scala at nine. My friend, Nene, can vouch for
me, along with the rest of the ensemble cast."

"Yes, that's right," I concurred. "We did not leave the theatre until three o'clock, when your constable came to see Renata."

"Hmm," said the Inspector. We intend to interview the domestic staff to see if they can shed any light on the situation."
Romano paused for a moment, fixing his steely gaze on Renata. "My constable checked with the hospital earlier this

morning, Signora Amato. Your husband is still poorly, but at least he is stable. So please try not to worry. Senior consultants can sometimes appear intimidating. But let me assure you that Ferrari is a skilled and dedicated doctor, well-liked and respected amongst his peers." Romano picked up his hat. "My sergeant and I will take our leave from you now. We know where you are if there are any pressing developments."

I left a note for Sherlock on his study desk, briefly explaining what had transpired, before Renata and I took a hansom to the Policlinico Hospital. When we arrived, we sat with Luigi, although he was asleep for much of the time. When he eventually awoke, he recognised his wife, smiling at her weakly. Then, unable to keep his eyes open any longer, Luigi drifted back into a deep sleep. Finally the Doctor told us to go home.

After dinner later that night, with still no word from my husband, I poured Renata and myself a Chianti, and she told me a little about her earlier life. Renata was adopted as a baby in Cremona, her place of birth, and then raised in the port city of Genoa by a well-to-do couple, Gustave and Agnese Cassuto, who were from Piedmont. Gustave was a self-made man who ran a successful shipbuilding yard at Varazze, where the Genoese Navy commissioned him to build sailing ships.

Renata had an idyllic childhood. She admitted that every whim was catered to, and she wanted for nothing. An only child, Renata was her parent's sole beneficiary when they tragically died in a train crash when she was seventeen. Renata inherited a small fortune, to be held in a trust fund until her upcoming twenty-fifth birthday on the fourth of August. She said she didn't care a jolt about the inheritance, explaining that all the money in the world could never compensate for the loss of her parents. There was a tear in her eye as she spoke of the accident that took their lives, along with that of

Renata's governess Benedetta, a widow. Renata and Benedetta's daughter, Giulia, were passengers on the same train, returning from a summer vacation in Rome. The girls were the only two in the carriage to escape with their lives, an episode so traumatic that Renata said the events of that dreadful day had haunted her ever since.

After the tragic death of Benedetta and her adoptive parents, Renata hired a private detective to find her birth parents. Sadly, she discovered her mother, Giorgia Rossi, had passed away years before from aggressive cancer. The irony was that she had moved to Bellagio after the adoption, where she lived less than four km from Milan for the remainder of her days. As for her biological father, Lorenzo Rossi, the detective revealed he was serving a life term in Milano jail for the murder of a child. After much deliberation, Renata decided not to pursue a relationship with him. Instead, Renata insisted that Giulia, who had no living relatives, stay with her. The girls, who were close in age, had grown up and played together since they were six, when Benedetta took up her position as a live-in governess. Renata told me she couldn't bear the thought of Giulia being left to fend for herself.

She explained that the girl fell out of an upstairs window when she was eight, sustaining a brain injury which developed into epilepsy grand mal. Consequently, she was often prone to fits and violent rages. The doctors wanted to commit Giulia to the asylum. Benedetta refused, and with the help of Renata's parents, Gustave and Agnese, they paid for Giulia's treatment at a private hospital. After that, for the most part, Giulia was fine, apart from the odd episode that flared up now and then. Realising that Giulia would find it hard to hold down a job elsewhere, Renata offered her friend a position. Eventually, Giulia took on the role of Renata's assistant and maid, a position she still held to this day. Renata said Giulia had been a diamond, a loyal servant who had helped her come to terms with her parents' demise. After being united in grief, the two women had reached a special understanding. Renata's compassion and kindness touched me deeply, I realised that a bond had slowly developed between us. Sophia was right—Renata was like a sister to me. I felt as protective of her as of one of my own family.

We were about to set off to the hospital on Sunday morning when there was a loud rapping on the front door. The maid entered the drawing room to announce that Inspector Romano was asking to see us. He burst into the parlour stony-faced, casting his dark eyes over the room. Romano admitted the Polizia hadn't got anywhere pursuing their lines of enquiry with Renata's domestic servants.

'We discovered that the strychnine kept in the outhouse used for pest control was missing,' said Romano. "Then we checked through Signor Amato's papers and discovered that someone recently took out an insurance policy on his life for ten thousand lire. A policy your husband claimed he knew nothing about."

Renata shook her head. "Luigi did not need life insurance, Inspector. We already have a substantial amount of money in trust, although those funds are not yet released."

The Inspector stared at Renata hard. We have checked with the Alleanza Assicurazioni Insurance Company, and they confirmed that you, Signora Amato, instructed them to start the policy.

Renata fell back in the chair as though struck by lightning. "But that is ridiculous. It is simply not true."

"Do you have a copy of the paperwork?" I quizzed. "So we could compare the signatures?"

"We have asked for the paperwork," said Romano. "Of course, as soon as we have it in hand we will compare the signatures. But, until that happens, you remain a person of interest. I must insist you give up your passport, Signora

Amato. Furthermore, you must not leave this city without my express permission. I hope you understand."

She glared at the Inspector, her eyes flashing with annoyance. "So, I am to be a suspect in my husband's suspected poisoning. I would never hurt Luigi, Inspector. If you think I would leave him in his hour of need, you are sadly mistaken. But, if this is how it is to be, then I will comply. Anything to bring the perpetrator to justice. Yet while you question my motives, the real culprit is still at large and must be brought to justice."

Romano wagged a precautionary finger. "Very well, but know this, Signora Amato. The clerk at the insurance company, Flavio Schiavo, recognised you. He said you left your gloves in his office. Schiavo ran outside, hoping to catch you, but found you getting into a carriage with a man who was not your husband. He knew this, of course, from having previously met Signor Amato."

"He is lying!" Renata flamed crimson. "There's not an iota of truth in those vile slurs. When was this transaction supposed to have been made? Give me dates!"

"Oh, I can assure you that we are looking into everything," said Romano. "Believe me, no stone will be left unturned." Romano stood and raised his hat. "I wish you ladies a good day. I will no doubt be in touch with you shortly." He placed a card on the table next to Renata. "I am not arresting you now, Signora Amato, due to your allegiance with Signora Sapori. But in the meantime, I suggest you engage the services of a reputable solicitor, because sadly I believe you are going to need one." And then, in a moment, Romano and his sergeant had left the room.

I glanced across at Renata. She looked exhausted, her eyes red from crying, the strain of grief etched upon her face. Someone was telling malicious stories about my friend. I instinctively knew her word was inviolate.

"Try not to worry," I said. "The evidence Romano has so far is mostly circumstantial, although the clerk's statement is of concern. Right, we need help." I rose.

"What are we to do now?" Renata wailed.

"I am taking you to the hospital to visit your husband. And then, my dear girl, I am going to make an appointment for us to see a solicitor."

CHAPTER FOUR: DUPLICITY

I dropped Renata off at the Policlinico Hospital and made my way to South Main Street, to the offices of Giovanni Marco. From what I could remember, he was a fussy little man with unruly hair and a pince-nez, albeit possessed of an exemplary reputation. Nevertheless, I was disappointed to learn he was in court and not expected to return that day. After giving some brief details to the receptionist, I made an appointment for Monday at one o'clock.

Afterwards, I checked in with the Poste Italiane telegraph office, but there was no message from Sherlock. By now, I was nearly out of my mind with concern. He was never one to rest his pen if he had something to say. I suspected the worst. What if something terrible had happened to him? I decided that if I did not hear from him by tomorrow, I would have no alternative but to report the matter to Romano.

I slipped back into the villa before collecting Renata from the hospital. I could hear my husband's voice ringing in my ear. *What have you overlooked, Nene? What's beyond doubt?*

From the drawing room, I glanced out the window and noticed a carriage waiting outside in the lane. A long black scarf concealed its driver's face. Then I saw something else that intrigued me further, the figure of a woman embarking from the bakery across the road. She looked remarkably like Renata and was laughing and joking with the driver in a girlish, carefree manner. She pecked him on the cheek, gazing at him adoringly. Finally, she flashed a wry smile before turning around and jumping into the carriage.

I ran outside onto the lane, but by the time I got there, the carriage and the shadowy figures had disappeared from view. I was shaking as I ran back into the villa in haste. I tripped over a footstool in the drawing room, but my fall was cushioned by the chaise lounge. Winded by the fall, I tried to get up when I felt strong arms lift me up onto my feet. I was about to cry out in protest until I recognised Sherlock's well-modulated voice. The relief I felt was immeasurable. I paused for a second, struggling to process the enormity of the moment. I felt a high of excitement, an adrenaline rush as I wrapped myself around my husband, holding onto him tightly.

"Thank God," I cried, kissing him firmly on the lips as I drank in his familiar scent.

Sherlock gently stroked my face before kissing me back passionately. "Well, that's singularly the nicest thing that's happened to me today. Tell me, are you hurt?" he asked, a concerned expression on his face.

I shook my head. "I have been so worried. You have no idea how I have longed to see you."

"I'm sorry I'm late. Please forgive me, but I got held up on an urgent case for Mycroft, although it proved not so urgent in the end. But, mind you, if I knew I would get this reaction from my wife, then perhaps I should arrive late more often."

"You are not funny," I retorted. "I am dealing with a crisis here—I have made an astonishing discovery."

"I am bracing myself for your revelation. Are the children all right?" he asked.

I could sense the concern and tension in his voice. I took a breath, relieved that I finally had my husband's full attention. We sat together on the chaise lounge, his hand in mine, as I explained all that had transpired with Renata, Luigi, and Inspector Romano, followed by the curious incident in the lane.

Sherlock excused himself and went outside into the lane. I watched through the window as my husband's keen eyes scoured the ground, looking for clues with the help of his magnifying glass. When he returned, he told me he had discovered the hoof prints of several horses that must have passed by that day, nothing sinister. He also discovered the footprints of two people. The larger one was from a man, a size eight, and the second footprint, with its deeper imprint into the soil, was smaller, size four, most likely having a spiked heel. Next to the footprint, my husband found a single red feather which he removed from his pocket, placing it into the palm of his hand.

"Well, this is obviously from a lady's hat," he said.

I nodded. "Yes, I remember now. The woman wore a red feather Bauer."

"Apart from that, alas, there was nothing remarkable about the scene." He shrugged.

I looked at my husband imploringly. "Sherlock, the woman I saw in the lane was *not* Renata. It would have been impossible for her to return from the hospital, change her clothes, and then arrive here in such a short time. None of this makes any sense. Please tell me you will speak to Romano. You cannot allow him to arrest my friend! I know the testimony of the insurance clerk does not look good. But please promise me you will keep Renata out of prison?"

"I will see what I can do. Was there a row or any altercation between the Amatos? How do you evaluate them as a couple?"

"No, not the slightest altercation at all. Sophia and I had dinner with them recently. Renata and Luigi are besotted with each other. Luigi is a charming man with an irreverent way with

words. He cuts quite a dash with the ladies. Tall, imposing, and darkly handsome. Any woman would be proud to call him her husband." I sighed. "Luigi does not underestimate the power of love."

"Does he not? Then God save us from such good men," Sherlock said stiffly, fixing me with his piercing eyes.

"Don't look at me like that. If I didn't know better, I'd think you were jealous, and I have never given you reason to be."

Sherlock raised an eyebrow. "I'm surprised you are such an ardent admirer of Amato's, given his reputation."

"I wouldn't go that far, I barely know him. But what do you mean by that? Because Luigi loves his wife and is not afraid to show his emotions, are you insinuating he is not to be trusted?"

"Something I heard from Lestrade about Amato's dubious reputation. There was quite a scandal in Covent Garden last year involving Amato and the married woman who played his leading lady. Her husband got wind of the affair and all hell let loose. Amato returned to Italy shortly afterwards. There was a rumour he was let go after he tried to force his attention on an understudy. It was all covered up at the time. So your friend may not be quite the loving husband he professes." He stared at me hard with his astute grey eyes. "As your husband, I grant you unconditional freedom. Still, I implore you not to be left alone in that man's company for any reason, unless of course you already have."

I narrowed my eyes, about to protest. Still, something in my husband's brusque manner, the way he looked at me with a furrowed brow, made me hesitate. I took a breath to collect my thoughts, but I couldn't stay silent any longer. "Sherlock, stop. You misunderstand. How can you think I was on intimate terms with Luigi Amato or that, God forbid, I would allow anything inappropriate to happen between us?"

He shook his head. "No, of course I don't think that. But it saddens me that you refuse to see Amato for what he is, a man with a dark heart."

"All right," I conceded. "Although I am shocked to hear what you say about Luigi, I know you speak the truth and I respect that as I respect you. But where does that leave Renata?"

"For the sake of your friendship with Renata Amato, I will endeavour to seek out the truth. Her husband undoubtedly has enemies. Whether any of them would wish him dead is another matter." Sherlock sighed. "I'm sorry, but it appears that our little rendezvous is on hold for now. But, on the face of it, this is an intriguing case, worthy of investigation."

He squeezed my hand, staring at me intently. "Nene, it's not feasible for one person to be in two places simultaneously. The likelihood of two people sharing so many facial features is also uncommon, but for them to show up in the same vicinity is remarkable. I shall ask Romano to send a constable to guard the house. I want you safe."

"Sherlock, you are starting to worry me."

"It is best to err on the side of caution. Prevention is always better than cure. I will need to go out shortly to see Romano and pursue further enquiries. When you return from the hospital with your friend, please stay in the villa until you hear from me. Promise you will do that?" For the first time, my husband sounded disturbed.

"Yes, Renata and I will comply, but what about the lawyer? We have an appointment with him on Monday."

"Cancel that for now. Hopefully your friend will not need one. It's unlikely I will return tonight, but please don't worry. I will message you in the morning." He paused for a moment. "Do you think it's wise to have your friend staying here with you?"

"Yes, I do. Renata has nowhere else to turn."

"All right, if you insist. I know how stubborn you can be, but we are a team, Nene. You and me. Remember, if you fall, I will catch you."

"Thank you for being so understanding. There was one other thing."

"Yes, what is it?" He smiled at me curiously. I knew from past experience that one glance from my husband was enough for him to know what was going on inside my head.

"I missed you, Sherlock, more than words can say. I am a strong independent woman, but I don't need protection from the Luigi Amatos of this world. I can take care of myself."

"Noted," said Sherlock with a bemused expression as I continued.

"As you know, I've had my fair share of difficult men, but you are my husband, not my saviour. You have no idea how much I long for you to be my husband right now." I stared at him expectantly.

He nodded. "You have been in my thoughts all day."

"Then prove it. I love you, Sherlock."

He smiled at me. "And who could blame you? But forgive me, I need to go. This is no time for intimacy. My primary concern is for you and the safety of our family. Don't worry, I promise I will make it up to you when I return."

"You'd better," I replied, before accepting a lingering kiss.

After Sherlock left, I sat on the chaise lounge for a while. Despite Sherlock's words of reassurance, I sensed a distance between us. Blinking at the ceiling, I tried desperately to process our earlier conversation. I couldn't believe my husband could think I was even remotely interested in Luigi Amato. During our conversation, I noticed Sherlock was not wearing his wedding ring. I knew he never wore it in London to avoid attracting attention, but I had never seen him without it in Italy. Now I had something else to worry about.

Finally, I set off to the hospital with our coachman Mattia to collect Renata. I could not help but wonder why Sherlock and I had been on the verge of an argument amidst a crisis. His insinuations had affected me deeply. Indeed, being with my husband was not without its challenges. He wasn't always pleasant to be around, and he could be difficult and prevaricating at times. Although we'd had some humdinger arguments in the past, we had never fallen out. Yet, for some inexplicable reason, my observations about Luigi Amato appeared to have vexed my husband and cast a dark shadow over our relationship. The idea of my infidelity was a ridiculous concept, for I had no interest in other men. I loved Sherlock dearly. But, on the other hand, perhaps I was reading too much into everything. There was probably a logical explanation about the ring. Sometimes your mind plays tricks, as my cousin Estelle was often keen to point out to me.

Nevertheless, I comforted myself in the knowledge that Sherlock, with his coherent and well-ordered mind, would come through for us. But, of course, my husband finds out everything in the end. A phenomenal observer, he was incredibly methodical, doggedly determined, and possessed the ability to solve the most complex crimes.

When Renata and I arrived back at the villa, I gently relayed all that had transpired. "Are you sure you don't have a doppelgänger?" I gently teased.

Renata shook her head. "I am an only child, as you are aware. But if someone is posing as me, then is it not possible this person may be responsible for forging the insurance policy and the attempted murder of my husband?"

I nodded in agreement. "My husband Lucca returned from London earlier today. He is making various enquiries on our behalf. He'll speak to Romano and ask for a constable to stay on guard outside the house."

"Thank you. I have no idea what I would have done without you. I have nowhere else to turn. My relatives are all dead, while my poor husband languishes in hospital."

Our conversation was interrupted by Renata's maid, Giulia, entering the room with a telegram for her mistress. My maid was away for a few days visiting her sick mother, so I'd gladly accepted Renata's request that Giulia stay with us until Luigi returned. Renata dismissed Giulia, patting her hand reassuringly and smiling at her knowingly before she left the room. Renata opened the telegram. It was from Ferrari. The Doctor informed Renata that her husband was now fully awake and lucid, and although he was still poorly, his vital signs looked promising. However, he still needed plenty of rest. Ferrari suggested we visit Luigi the following day after he completed his final assessment.

Renata collapsed into my arms.

"Well, that's excellent news," I said. "All we need to do now is find the perpetrator. With my husband and Inspector Romano on the case, we'll be sure to do so soon."

Renato brightened at my narrative. We had an early dinner that night before retiring to the patio, where we were attended to by Giulia. I struck up a conversation with her, attempting to get to know and understand this girl who was such an important part of Renata's life. Giulia was a tall slim young lady with an amenable personality, exceedingly pretty with a lightly freckled face, expressive blue eyes covered with thick-rimmed glasses, and her lovely flaming red hair tied up in a neat bun.

Guilia explained how she loved working for Signora Amato, a position she said she was grateful to have after being left alone in the world.

Renata and I sat on the patio, watching the sun go down until the moon rose and the night sky turned nocturnally blue, shimmering between the green leaves of the olive branches. We chatted for some time until, utterly exhausted, we retired for the night.

Chapter Five: Love and Infidelity

R enata appeared in much better spirits at breakfast the following morning. However, she refused to stay in the
house, explaining she desperately needed to be at the hospital
when Ferrari completed his assessment. I didn't even try to
dissuade her. I would have done the same if, God forbid, anything ever happened to Sherlock.

I slipped outside to speak to the constable, and he kindly
agreed to accompany us to the hospital.

We sat in the waiting room until, eventually, Ferrari appeared to relay the good news that there seemed to be no col-
lateral damage to Luigi's internal organs. So first, they'd put
him on a positive pressure device to help restore his respira-
tory drive. Then, provided he continued to breathe unaided
for the next forty-eight hours, Luigi would be allowed to
come home.

"Your husband has been very fortunate." Ferrari smiled
warmly at Renata. "He is what the English say... the cat with
nine lives."

Renata laughed, throwing her arms around the startled
medic. "Thank you so much, from the bottom of my heart.
May I see Luigi now?"

"I don't see why not," said Ferrari. "My nurse will take you
to him."

We accompanied the nurse into the ward, where Renata
and Luigi were reunited. I left them alone and sat in the waiting room, contemplating the day's events. I pondered how
Sherlock and Romano were getting on trying to track down

the perpetrator.

Renata was finally shooed out of the ward by the nurse, who said Signor Amato needed to rest, and our lovely constable took us back to the Villa. We chatted over dinner. I was delighted to find Renata in a more amenable mood. We sat up until late, chatting about opera, life, and love. The more time I spent in Renata's company, the more I liked her. I felt as though I could talk to her about anything. Finally, Renata made her excuses and retired for the evening.

Despite the late hour, I decided to wait for Sherlock, as I would be unable to sleep until I knew he was safely home. So I felt relieved when he eventually arrived at eleven o'clock. I poured us a drink, and he urged me to update him on the events that had transpired so far, although I could still sense the tension between us from his manner and the tone of his voice.

"Is everything all right?" I quizzed.

Sherlock did not answer my question. Instead, he asked another. "What did you say to Sophia Moon?" he snapped.

"What on earth do you mean? I didn't say anything. Where has this come from?"

"I bumped into your friend earlier today. She told me, in no uncertain terms, how upset you were. She then took great delight in lecturing me on my catastrophic failings as a husband and a father. As you can imagine, it was quite a lengthy conversation."

"That must have been taxing for you," I said, thinking how I would have loved to have been a fly on the wall.

"The conversation was surprisingly enlightening. Sophia Moon told me how I overthink too much and perceive far too little. A wife seeks compassion and understanding from her husband, not an analytical lecture."

"Look, Sophia got hold of the wrong end of the stick. The last time I saw her, I may have mentioned that I was upset because you forgot to message me as arranged. I swear it was nothing more. I have never discussed our private life with anyone." I crossed my fingers, thinking of the nights Sophia and I sat up discussing life and love over a glass of wine.

"What is done is done."

"How did you respond to Sophia?" I asked with some trepidation.

"I told the young lady she should get her affairs in order before poking her nose into my personal life. People in glass houses shouldn't throw stones."

"What did you mean by that?"

Sherlock paused before responding. "Something I discovered at Simpson's last week at dinner. I saw Moon in the restaurant with a woman. He did not recognise me, as he was far too busy gazing into the eyes of the lady in question. And before you ask, it was not his wife nor anyone I recognised."

"Well, Robert does have a female assistant."

Sherlock rolled his eyes. "That's one way of putting it. Tell me, what does this so-called assistant look like?"

"Well, let me see. Robert's assistant Mia would be in her mid-twenties, attractive, tall, slim, blonde with blue eyes."

"You describe her admirably."

"Oh, my god. Please tell me you did not say anything to Sophia."

"Of course not. Although I was sorely tempted after my interrogation. No, I'm afraid that's your job, Nene. It should come from you. Sophia Moon is your best friend. Although I did notice Moon's hand was shaking slightly. I suggest he consult a doctor to rule out any underlying illnesses."

"All right," I conceded. "I will mention it to Sophia. However, I'm finding it hard to believe that Robert would cheat on his wife. I pray they manage to work it out. There are two children to consider."

"This woman you saw in the lane, tell me again what was

different about her. Please try to remember, as it could be crucial."

"Her smile was strange, almost childlike, bordering on sardonic. She wore a cloak over her dress, so it was difficult to tell what she was wearing underneath, but I remember now that it was her walk that gave it away. Her walk was different."

"Please clarify."

"She wore red heels, something I've never seen Renata wear. She confided in me that she could not abide heels. Renata has a high instep, making it difficult for her to walk in them."

"Well done. You paint a compelling picture. Now, at last, we are getting somewhere. Not only do you see, but you now observe. Please describe your friend to me. Give me as much detail as possible."

"But, Sherlock, you will see her for yourself tomorrow."

"No matter. I wish to hear her description from you."

So I explained Renata to my husband as best I could, careful not to omit any details.

"Where did Renata Amato's biological mother give birth?"

"Cremona. Renata told me she was adopted at the Della Speranza orphanage. Her mother's name was Giorgia Rossi. Why, do you think it's important?"

"I think it's highly relevant. I realise we have much lost time to make up. But forgive me, for I must leave you again first thing."

"But Sherlock, I've hardly seen you. Tell me, when can I expect you to return?"

"I will be with you as soon as I can. So don't worry, I will message you shortly. In the meantime, while I am away, please take good care. And be sure to ask the servants to lock all the doors and windows before you go to bed. Promise me you will do that?"

"All right, I will, I promise. Can I get you another drink?" I quizzed.

"A whiskey and soda would be most welcome. Oh, and for future reference, if I unintentionally do or say anything to make you upset, or if you become unhappy with our arrangement for any reason then you must tell me. So I can address the situation without involving a third party."

I took a breath. "Sherlock, I have two questions."

"Name them."

"Do you want a divorce?"

"And the second question?"

"Do you still see your future with me?"

Sherlock let out a deep sigh before answering. "No to the first, and yes to the second." He paused. "Nene, you're an incredible woman. You are a knot I would never want to untie."

"Not bad, husband, not bad at all." I whispered, almost to myself. "Could you please say that again?"

"I'm not going to repeat myself, you heard perfectly well the first time. When we married, I promised I would be with you until the end. And this is not the end."

"Sherlock, you know I would never cheat. My heart beats only for you and the children."

"I should hope so, too. After my altercation with Sophia Moon, I may be scarred for life." He hesitated for a moment. "And Nene, ditto." He kissed me gently as he gazed into my eyes, cupping my chin in his hand. "Is it all getting to be too much for you? Do you want me to give up detective work? Because I will if you ask."

I shook my head. "No, not at all. You would be miserable, then so would I. Besides, who am I to deprive the world of its greatest living consulting detective? I can cope with your absences, Sherlock. But don't shut me out. You said we are a team. So please allow me to help you and my friend. I want to do that for Renata."

He squeezed my hand and smiled tenderly. "All right, if you insist. I suppose even Sherlock Holmes needs help sometimes." He stared at me curiously. "How do you feel about coming with me tomorrow to visit Cremona?"

I looked at Sherlock in astonishment as he explained what he wanted us to do, thrilled he still had faith in me. We sat together, sipping our drinks. I was happy we were back on track, at least for now. Although I couldn't stop thinking of Sophia. I knew it must have taken a lot to confront my husband after being on the receiving end of his acid tongue in the past. But even so, I knew I had to put her right while at the same time broaching the subject of her husband's infidelity. I wasn't looking forward to that conversation.

I poured another glass of wine and sat back in my chair as we listened to Schubert, reflecting on some of the times I had spent with Sophia, most notably an evening at my villa in Milan nearly seven years ago, just a few weeks after Sherlock and I returned from our honeymoon in Paris. Sophia was naturally curious to hear about Paris. It is such an incredible city. It possesses all the qualities one would wish for a honeymoon — amazing food, outstanding beauty, breath-taking architecture, splendid grandeur, and fabulous fashion. Arguably not quite on a par with Milan, but still magnificent. Many have described Paris as the capital of the nineteenth century. I was so excited when Sherlock and I arrived there in the summer of 1899.

The first night of our honeymoon was a strange affair, however. Sherlock and I had become lovers four years previously, our union resulting in the arrival of our much-wanted son, Nicco. Even so, for some inexplicable reason, we were initially a little shy around each other once we were married. Once we'd retired to our suite for the night, I remember the clear starlight August evening and my new husband's apprehension. However, the trees gently shimmering in the light breeze and the flickering of the taper candles helped put me at ease.

Finally, I had invited Sherlock to sit on the balcony to watch the sunset. To lighten the mood, I poured us each a glass of champagne. We'd chatted for a while, like old times, until, eventually, the atmosphere became more relaxed as we got our bearings and exchanged shy lingering glances. Then, finally, I stood and kissed him gently on the cheek, suggesting he enjoy a last cigarette and finish his drink before joining me in the bedroom.

He had looked at me oddly for a moment before nodding in agreement.

I'd watched, smiling, as he removed his silver cigarette case from his pocket before I made my way to the bedroom. There I quickly changed into a midnight blue silk nightgown. I untied my hair, and brushed it before letting it hang loose over my shoulders. Then I sat on the bed and waited nervously for my husband to join me.

This would be the first time since Fiesole that we'd been in such proximity to one another, so I'd figured it would take time to become used to each other's idiosyncrasies and habits again. As a consequence, my expectations were not too high. I decided to play a little game — my accomplice, a box of Swan Vestas matches.

Sherlock eventually entered the room. He'd given me a withering glance as he sat on the edge of the bed. "This is ridiculous nonsense. Give me my matches, please. I know you have them." He leaned across, taking hold of my hand in an attempt to retrieve the little box I had hidden under the pillow. A deep furrow etched between his dark eyebrows, he opened my palm and appeared surprised to find it empty. My other hand reached out to stroke his face. I took a sharp intake of breath as his stubble brushed my skin. I couldn't help but laugh, observing his perplexed expression.

"I don't think you want to do this," I'd whispered.

A faint smile appeared on my husband's face. "Oh, but I do," he growled, pulling me to him. The feral look he gave me unnerved and excited me simultaneously. And then, in a moment, his mouth was on mine, pressing down urgently.

Sherlock's eyes had sought mine, his face suffused with a passion I recognised from the first time we lay together. Observing the vulnerability of such a physically strong man was an overwhelming experience. He never once took his eyes off me as I slowly removed my nightgown and unbuttoned his shirt, staring at him expectantly. Finally, he let out a groan of appreciation, staring at my naked form.

"Dio Mio, you are a grand woman," he whispered.

I'd smiled. It was still there after all this time — that unbridled passion that first flamed in Fiesole now reignited. To be with him this way was exhilarating. When our union was over, I lay in his arms. I realised this man I loved was unlike any of the men I had known before him. Although I couldn't figure out which particular thing set him apart from other men. I looked at him as he drifted off into sweet slumber, thinking how beautiful he was.

When we open ourselves up to loving someone, we immediately become vulnerable. The moment we feel protected, we are inevitably exposed to the risk of losing that protection. But with Sherlock, I decided that was a risk I was willing to take.

When I had completed my story, I'd turned to see Sophia's raised eyebrows. She'd appeared somewhat shocked at my revelations. "When I was a young girl, Mother drummed into me and my sister Ornella that it was unladylike to smoke cigarettes in public, we were only to drink wine in moderation, and we were never to be seen with a man without a chaperone." She shook her head. "As for carnal pleasure, that was completely out of the question outside marriage. And even then having intercourse was seen as a duty for procreation, not pleasure. Being happily married was not a requirement.

Mother said Ornella and I were to protect our virtue at all costs. She told us that a mere glimpse of a man's nether regions was enough to render us pregnant. But then I fell in love with Robert and realised how ridiculous that was. Robert encouraged me to be open about my sexual preferences. He taught me that desire is a deliberate emotion driven by nature and too important to ignore. But, being older, Robert was far more experienced in such matters than me."

"Yes," I'd agreed. 'As my husband correctly pointed out, sexual intimacy is a free source of pleasure. In addition, it lowers stress levels and helps with insomnia. So what's not to like?'

"Trust Holmes to find a practical side to the pleasures of the marriage bed." Sophia had giggled.

As Sherlock and I climbed the stairs to bed, I prayed that Sophia and Robert would find a way to reconcile. Then my thoughts took me back to Renata and her mother. I felt excited at the prospect of investigating with my husband. I knew he was certain something of relevance would be found in Cremona. My husband would be out by the first light on the morrow, pursuing inquiries. We arranged to meet later that morning at Milano Centrale station.

Chapter Six: The Tragic Death of Pedro Endrizzi

R omano called at the villa the following morning, just as Renata was about to set off to the hospital. He said La Scala confirmed Signora Amato had been rehearsing on the morning of the twelfth of June, the day the insurance papers were signed. In addition, the signature on the insurance documents had proven inconclusive. The police were now looking for a third party to help them with their enquiries. Renata was, of course, delighted with the news. Out of curiosity, she checked the date in her house diary. She gazed at the entry, a puzzled expression on her face.

Renata explained she'd had a doctor's appointment on the twelfth. When she'd mentioned this to her husband at breakfast the day before, Luigi had asked her to take a parcel to the post office, a present for an old friend, as he would be away on business and was not expected to return until the following evening. Renata happily agreed to her husband's request, but before breakfast on the day in question, she received a telephone call from the artistic director at La Scala begging her to go in.

He said they had some critical scenes to rehearse that required her presence. Furthermore, he explained they were already behind schedule. So Renata reluctantly agreed to cancel her doctor's appointment, as it was only a routine matter. Then when she'd arrived at La Scala, she asked her coachman to take the parcel into town. She never bothered mentioning it to her husband, as she thought the matter was far too trivial.

Before Renata and the constable left for the hospital, I told her of my plans to travel to Cremona with my husband, although, on Sherlock's instructions, I didn't divulge the reason why. Renata reassured me that she would be fine with Giulia to keep her company and the constable offering her protection, although I noticed she raised an eyebrow when I revealed our destination.

"I sincerely hope you find what you are looking for." She kissed me fondly on the cheek and squeezed my hand as our hansom dropped me off at Milano Centrale station.

I found Sherlock waiting when I arrived, a solitary figure impatiently pacing up and down the platform. He acknowledged my presence with a smile and a nod. We caught the train to Stazione of Cremona, arriving at our destination at noon. From there, we took another cab to di Stato di Cremona. A wealthy industrial city and the custodian of some of the most exemplary mediaeval architecture, it was also the home of the orphanage Il Noto Orfanotrofio Della Speranza. We looked ahead as the carriage drove up the tree-lined drive towards its imposing front door. I shuddered at the façade. This drab, stone-grey building looked more like a prison than an orphanage.

The director and orphan keeper, Madius Muller, ushered us into his office. He was expecting us, as we had messaged him the day before. Muller was a sombre middle-aged man of diminutive build, with a handlebar moustache and a firm handshake. He offered coffee, and we gladly accepted. Sherlock explained how my friend Renata was adopted and gave the director her mother's name and year of birth. Muller took a leather-bound journal from a bookcase and placed it on his desk. The journal was dated 1880. Muller's fingers stopped at a page.

He showed us the entry dated the fourth of August. "It is a

sad reflection of our times that one-third of babies born in Florence and Milan are abandoned every year at foundling homes such as this one. At the time we were so overrun with unwanted children that the authorities didn't know what to do with them. I'm afraid life is still desperately hard for many." He glanced at the picture of a baby girl, Renata, as an infant. "This child was one of the lucky ones. She was adopted soon after this picture was taken. But her mother, Giorgia Rossi, did not abandon her. Sadly, she had little choice. Her husband was in prison, and with no relatives to help or other visible means of support, her only option was to give the child up for adoption."

"Is that a birthmark?" Sherlock keenly pointed to the picture of the baby. He stared at it closely and drew attention to a small mark in the shape of a strawberry on the infant's neck.

Muller nodded. "Indeed. The child was born with infantile hemangioma. She was a bonnie wee thing." He sighed.

"The irony is the child's biological father, Lorenzo Rossi, was recently released from San Vittore prison with a full pardon. After he protested his innocence for years, a witness finally collaborated his story."

"Wasn't Rossi supposed to have killed a child?" Sherlock asked.

"Yes," agreed Muller. "His employer's son, Pedro Endrizzi, who was found bludgeoned to death in the garden of his home. The Endrizzis employed Rossi as a gardener and handyman. Pedro's father, Angelo, arrived home from work to find Rossi covered in blood, hovering over his son's body. The police arrested Rossi. Despite his protestations, explaining he was only trying to help the boy, no one believed him. Rossi was subsequently tried and convicted of second-degree murder."

"So who was the witness that came forward?" Sherlock quizzed.

"It was Pedro's brother, Milo. He backed Rossi's story. You see, he could not live with the guilt. For it was his mother, Elisheba, who'd committed the crime. She was known for being fiery-tempered, always quick to fly off the handle. One morning, Pedro and his mother argued in the kitchen. Elisheba was in a particularly foul mood. She'd been drinking heavily. After Pedro refused to do what she asked, Elisheba picked up the poker and chased her son out into the garden. Pedro fell and hit his head on a rock. Elisheba, intoxicated with gin, was worked up into a frenzy and hit her son repeatedly. Until that moment, Milo was blissfully unaware that a heated domestic drama was unfolding downstairs, but then he witnessed the scene from his bedroom window. By the time he ran downstairs, Rossi had arrived and tried to comfort the boy and stem the bleeding, but it was already too late." Muller shook his head. "Angelo arrived at the scene as his son drew his last breath. When Milo tried to tell his father what happened, he swore his son to silence, coercing the boy into getting his story straight. Despite what she had done, Angelo covered for his wife, but not out of love. No, he didn't want to be left alone having to raise his other children. You see, Angelo was having an affair and didn't want his family to get in the way of his newfound love. So Milo, who was fourteen at the time, was forced to make a statement to the police and convince everyone that Rossi was responsible for his brother's death. Pedro was barely ten years old when his mother cruelly ended his life."

"And where is the mother now?" I asked.

"Elisheba passed away recently in a psychiatric hospital, no doubt driven mad with grief. The family had already disbanded. Angelo immigrated to Australia, abandoning his wife and family for his lover. Eventually, Milo's siblings moved away. His sister married a wine merchant from Lombardy, while his brother won a scholarship at La Fenice

Theatre School in Venice. The family eventually lost touch. So when Milo was recently diagnosed with leukaemia, he decided to come forward to do the right thing."

I stared at Muller in stunned disbelief. "My god, what a heart-wrenching story. Those poor children, how they must have suffered. But how can you know all this about Milo Endrizzi? "

Muller smiled at me gently. "My sister Leba is a matron at the infirmary in Cremona. She works in the oncology ward, where Milo was a patient. Over time they became friends, and Milo confided in Leba. She helped him to put his affairs in order. My sister even arranged for a lawyer to prepare his last will. But, sadly, the poor man has only weeks left at the most."

"Is the infirmary far from here?" asked Sherlock.

Muller shook his head. "Milo recently transferred to a private ward at the Ospedale Maggiore in Milan, known as the Policlinico Hospital. My sister said they have better facilities and they would be able to make him more comfortable in his final days. Milo has the means and money to pay." Muller cocked his head, smiling at us curiously. "You must be familiar with the establishment, Signor and Signora Sapori?"

I nodded in agreement. "Yes, my friend's husband is a patient at the Policlinico. We are aware of its excellent reputation."

We finished our coffee. Then, finally, Sherlock thanked Muller for his assistance. Before we left, he told us that Lorenzo Rossi was thought to be living in Como. We decided not to travel back to Milan straight away. I told Sherlock we needed to spend some time together. He agreed to my request. Moreover, my husband knew that as much as I loved and respected him, I would never hesitate to challenge him over something I strongly believed in. He described it as my wonton stubbornness.

Instead, we took a room at The Black Bear Inn after I finally persuaded my reluctant husband to travel to Como the following day to try and track down Renata's birth father, Lorenzo Rossi. However, I was somewhat perplexed by his lack of enthusiasm.

We explored Cremona in the afternoon, the birthplace of Antonio Stradivari. There was a museum in Stradivari's honour, the Museo Del Violino, that we intended to visit. First, I persuaded Sherlock to visit the cathedral. Its bell tower, the famous Torrazzo, was the city's symbol and the tallest in Italy. The interior was as breathtaking as its exterior, housing several essential works of art. The oldest were the frescoes of the stories of Abraham, Isaac, Jacob, and Joseph, held in the Southern and Northern transept vaults. However, the most highly symbolic artistic creation of the cathedral was the fresco decoration on the side walls of the nave portraying the life of Mary and Christ. We sat for some time, marvelling at its intrinsic beauty.

I lit a candle and prayed, Sherlock waiting for me patiently, before we entered the Piazza Del Comune, a picturesque square in the heart of the city, said to be the most charming in Italy and the focus of the city's social, cultural, and political activities. Its well-preserved historic buildings have witnessed Cremona's tumultuous life throughout the centuries.

We ordered Gravina wine and a jug of water. Sipping our drinks, we watched the tourists walk by and admire the stunning architecture while we tried to digest Muller's extraordinary story. Sherlock sat back in his chair, his long legs stretched before him, and looked at me languidly.

"I'm glad you are here with me, Nene. I wish to apologise for being distant and creating awkwardness between us." He sighed. "I am a jealous, possessive man who did not consider your feelings, and I am truly sorry for that jealousy. After all these years, you must know what I'm like. But despite what you might think of me and all my foibles, I remain undeniably romantically in love with you."

"It's all right, I understand." I squeezed his hand, relieved I finally had my husband back.

I couldn't help staring at Sherlock, he looked so handsome. I felt so blessed to be here with him like this. Over the years, he had brought much-needed calm and stability into my life. I'd even managed to forge a relationship with his brother Mycroft. Although I never once took our relationship for granted, the words Mycroft had conveyed so eloquently in Fiesole ten years ago would remain forever indelibly imprinted on my mind. I reminded myself that despite my husband's protestations to the contrary, a day could arrive when he would tire of domestic bliss. And I knew that if that day came, I would be hurt immeasurably and I would be bereft. However, part of me would understand, and until that time, I was determined to make the most of things. But now, sitting here with him, I felt invincible.

"Another bottle of wine, please. So we can relax." Sherlock gestured to the waiter.

"That would be most welcome." I sighed. Glancing down, I noticed my husband wore his wedding ring. "Had you mislaid it?" I raised an eyebrow, gesturing to the third finger on Sherlock's left hand.

"Ah, this." He said, twisting the ring around on his finger. "I appear to have gained a little weight recently. Mrs Hudson's cooking and too many dinners at Simpson's no doubt. The ring became a little tight, so I took it into the jewellers and had it loosened."

We sat on the square in the glorious afternoon sun, partaking in wine, bread, olives, and dolce latte, catching up on our news and chatting about the children. Eventually we returned to discussing the case and our findings at the orphanage. Sherlock admitted he was apprehensive about travelling to Como on the morrow to try and track down Renato's birth father.

"But why?"

"Because I'm afraid that when we discover the truth, you may wish we hadn't. But for the sake of your friendship with Renata Amato, I fear we have little choice."

"Thank you, I love you for that." Tears stung my eyes. "I know you'll do everything you can to vindicate Renata." I was determined to do anything to help prove my friend innocent.

We took a stroll after our drinks, stopping off to check out the Museo del Violino, where we discovered there would be a recital of "Il Suono Di Stradivari" later that night. We booked two tickets before returning to the hotel to take a siesta before dinner. However we didn't get much sleep. Instead, we spent the remainder of the afternoon chatting and recapturing our physical closeness in the way only lovers can.

A cool breeze wafted through the blinds, embracing our naked bodies in the glow of the afternoon sun. My husband derived pleasure from serenity. It settled him for a while, but in the back of my mind, I knew he needed drama and tension to keep his great brain active, like a drug he constantly craved.

CHAPTER SEVEN: THE ABSOLUTION OF LORENZO ROSSI

After breakfast the following morning, Sherlock and I set out on our journey to Como. Travelling by train, we arrived at our destination at 11:30. Muller told us Lorenzo Rossi was rumoured to be working as a potman at the San Carlo inn, so we decided to have an early luncheon there.

The Inn was unpretentious, with an outdoor seating area and an established garden offering spectacular views over the lake. Sherlock ordered a cold beer and a glass of Friulano for me, which was surprisingly good. Its silky palate of delicate flowers and slightly bitter almond finish were refreshing. We ordered chicken and the Columbian salad. Our waitress was Olivia, the wife of the owner, Umberto Berlusconi. Olivia had a friendly disposition and was well-built, with dark hair and sparkling brown eyes. Sherlock asked Olivia if Lorenzo Rossi was working that day.

"Yes, Lorenzo is on duty in the cellar. He is due for a break shortly. Would you like me to send for him?"

"Thank you. My name is Lucca Sapori. Signor Rossi does not know me by name, but please tell him I am a friend of his daughter."

Olivia smiled and nodded, collecting our empty plates before returning to the Inn to pass on the message. We waited patiently for ten minutes, then noticed a man walking toward us, his head bowed and his shoulders stooped. He looked to be around fifty — tall, slim, with grey receding hair and eyes as black as ebony. The man removed his cap as he approached the table and flashed a gap-toothed smile before introducing himself as Lorenzo Rossi. Sherlock gestured for Lorenzo to take a seat. He hesitated for a moment, before taking a chair at the table.

Sherlock pushed a glass of cold beer toward him and began telling him that we were friends of his daughter Renata. Then, finally excusing himself, explaining he had to get back to work, Lorenzo agreed to meet with us later that afternoon to continue our discussion at The Albergo Firenze hotel, where Sherlock and I had booked a suite on the first floor. The hotel was in the centre of Como, within 600 metres of the lake shores. Sherlock and I took a stroll there that afternoon, soaking up the atmosphere and the stunning scenery, arriving back at our hotel in ample time to greet our guest.

Lorenzo arrived at five p.m. He had changed out of his work clothes into a black sack suit and a white shirt with a rounded collar. Although his face was heavily lined, I imagined he must have been a handsome man in his younger days. He removed his cap as the bellboy ushered him into our suite, looking around nervously as Sherlock greeted him warmly and invited him to take a seat. Pushing a glass of whisky and a plate of sandwiches towards Lorenzo, I watched as he relaxed after a few sips from his glass. He devoured the sandwiches hungrily, wiping his chin with a napkin.

Lorenzo spoke of his earlier life, when he was wrongly incarcerated in Milano prison for a crime he said he did not commit. His wife, Giorgia, whom he loved dearly, visited him there. She was heavily pregnant, and with no money or relatives to help, they reluctantly agreed to put their child up for adoption, although they were heartbroken at the prospect. Lorenzo said his devout wife never got over losing her child. Giorgia's cancer two years later was yet another terrible wrench, and she suffered greatly before she passed away.

Nevertheless, Lorenzo noted that as dead as she was, his wife meant more to him than any other living woman. When he was finally released from prison with a full pardon, he moved to Como where he took the position of cellar man with the Berlusconis and lived in a room above the Inn. He said he was content with his life, having struck up a close friendship with two co-workers.

"What of my girl?" Lorenzo asked. "Please tell me about her."

Sherlock relayed to Lorenzo how Renata had a happy childhood. He spoke of her adoptive parents' untimely demise, and her talent as an opera singer and her subsequent marriage to Luigi Amato. Sherlock explained that although Renata was initially a suspect in the attempted murder of her husband, she was exonerated as the evidence had proved inconclusive.

Lorenzo stared at Sherlock imploringly. "Please keep my daughter safe, Mr Sapori. I have no time for the police with the way they persecuted me. I don't want Renata to end up like me, wrongly imprisoned for a crime she did not commit. But, Signor Sapori, do you believe my daughter is innocent?"

"Yes, I do. I would stake my reputation on it."

Lorenzo nodded. "Then that's good enough for me."

"Lightning seldom strikes twice." Sherlock smiled grimly. "You have my word that I will do everything possible to protect your daughter's reputation and bring the real perpetrator to justice."

Lorenzo gazed at Sherlock with a perplexed expression. "But aren't you going to ask me if I did it? If I killed that boy?"

Sherlock shook his head. "I know you didn't murder Pedro Endrizzi. My wife and I learned about the brother's testimony."

Lorenzo nodded. "You're a good man, Signor Sapori. I could never lay my hands on an innocent child. Do you and your wife have children?

"Yes," said Sherlock. "We were blessed with a son and a daughter."

Lorenzo smiled. "Then keep them close. Not everyone is so fortunate. When you see my daughter, please be sure to tell her that I was proven innocent of the crime. However, I am prepared to walk away if she refuses to see me. But If she agrees, then send the word, and I will come at once to meet her in Milan."

Finally, the men shook hands, and in a moment Lorenzo had left the building. Sherlock sighed deeply.

"I think we should go out for dinner. I'm sure we could both use a drink."

We arrived back in Milan by late afternoon the following day. Over dinner, I introduced Sherlock to Renata as my husband, Lucca Sapori. We explained all that had transpired with Lorenzo, his wrongful imprisonment, subsequent pardon, and how much he longed to meet his daughter. Renata burst into tears. But they were tears of joy and happiness. Renata said she was thrilled her father had been proven innocent. She was looking forward to finally meeting him. Furthermore, she had something else to celebrate—Luigi would be home the following day. The doctors were delighted with his recovery. Renata finally retired for the night with a smile on her face and a happy heart.

I awoke the following morning and came downstairs to find my husband dressed and taking coffee in the morning room, seemingly engrossed in his newspapers.

"Have you had breakfast?" I quizzed.

"Did you say something?" he grunted, not once looking up from his papers.

"It doesn't matter. Someone's grumpier than usual this morning." I sighed before walking out of the room.

I joined Renata for breakfast before she left to go to the hospital. The Amatos and Giulia would return to their own residence later that afternoon.

Sherlock eventually joined me at the breakfast table. "Forgive me if I've been distracted. I have to go out shortly, but I will be back before dinner." He looked at me curiously. "You have changed your perfume?"

"Yes, it's jasmine. Do you like it?"

"It's very nice, but I prefer the other one." He leaned over and kissed my neck, gently stroking my hair.

His words punctuated the tender look that only a ten-year-old marriage can evoke. "Give me your hat," I said, watching as my husband pulled on his jacket.

"Why? What's wrong with it?" He chuckled.

"It's dusty. No self-respecting wife would allow her husband to be seen in a dusty hat." I lovingly brushed it before handing it back to him, much to my husband's amusement.

Once Sherlock left for the day, I was alone in the house, apart from the servants. So I sent my coachman a note for Sophia, inviting her to luncheon. She arrived at noon wearing a beautiful pink silk dress, a sombre expression clouding her lovely face. After we ate, we took coffee in the garden surrounded by baskets and tubs spilling over with flowers and greenery. We were disturbed only by the chirping of two black redstarts perched overhead in the olive trees. I gently quizzed my friend about her altercation with my husband.

Sophia looked at me sheepishly as she took a sip from her cup. "I'm sorry, Nene, but given the opportunity, I felt compelled to confront Sherlock. I knew how much he had upset you."

"Sophia, it was a simple misunderstanding between a husband and wife. You had no right to interfere."

Sophia paused, considering her words carefully. Throughout our conversation, she appeared on the edge of tears. "You once told me that you developed a crush on Sherlock from the first time you saw him standing under the streetlamp in Baker Street."

I nodded. "Yes, that's true. That feeling has never left me, even after all these years. When we reconciled in Milan, you thought I was settling for a man who could never be completely mine, but you were wrong, Sophia. I never settled. I have learned from being with my husband that love isn't always rational and sensible, it cannot always make sense. Friendship, on the other hand, what I have with you, is no different. We choose to spend time with people we love and regard as friends because they enhance our lives. Love isn't an ultimate state, it's an act of courage and an uphill struggle sometimes. I reached out to Sherlock as I reached out to you, Sophia. There is a difference between compromise and sacrifice."

"Yes, there is also a difference between tenacity and despair. Still, I suppose nothing motivates one like love and reason, described by some as the higher form of passion. Although at the same time, I am ashamed to say that sometimes when I see you and Sherlock together, I feel resentment, and I am jealous of how you light up in each other's presence, although he's rarely in it. That man does not deserve you."

I sighed. "Sophia, it's not always that simple. Not having my husband constantly by my side doesn't mean I seek commiseration. I am not a conundrum to be resolved. Love is being with someone who understands you inside and out. When I look at Sherlock, I see only the best in him. And for the sake of our friendship, I implore you to do the same."

Sophia nodded. "I will try for your sake, Nene. I am sorry if I've caused you any distress. Sadly, the gloss has gone from my marriage. When Robert returned from London, he confessed to having an affair with his assistant, Mia. He swears it's over, but I don't feel as though I can trust him again. He told me he made a mistake." She sighed. "A mistake is putting on the wrong tie or forgetting to fasten your shoelaces. Robert knew what he was doing. That man has made a mockery of our marriage. So I told him I wanted a divorce."

I stared at my friend, tears in my eyes. "I weep for you, Sophia. But tell me, do you still love Robert?"

"It's complicated.'

"No, it's not," I retorted. "You either love him or you don't. It's quite straightforward."

"And what if I do?"

"Then you must fight for him. He is your husband, the father of your children. It won't be easy. It will require effort on both sides. But it's not too late to recapture what you had. Although there is one thing I should tell you."

"And what is that?"

"Sherlock saw them together — Robert and Mia — having dinner at Simpson's."

Sophia furrowed her brow. "What else did the celebrated detective have to say?"

"Sherlock suggested Robert be seen by a physician. He noticed his hand shook when he raised his glass."

Sophia sighed. A single tear fell down her cheek. "I will quiz my philandering husband and insist he see a doctor, but since his father died six months ago, Robert has not been himself. The grief he endured was a visceral blow. He has been moody and irritable of late, and he's been drinking heavily. I haven't said anything I thought it was my husband's way of dealing with the situation. Love," she scoffed. "You forget how easy the first flush is until it gets overcomplicated with things of little or no relevance. When people marry, they pledge to live together in harmony 'till death. But no one can maintain that facade indefinitely, it's impossible."

"Yes," I agreed. "But I have seen you with Robert — the way he gets under your skin, your shining love for one another.

Love takes comprehension and understanding. A spiteful word or action from a stranger will never sting like it does when executed by someone we love." I took Sophia's hand in mine. "You need to talk to Robert. Would you like me to act as a go-between?"

Sophia shook her head. "No, that won't be necessary. I shall speak to Robert this evening when he returns from La Scala. I will see what I can salvage from our relationship. Although I'm not sure I can get past his infidelity whether he is ill or not. Would you forgive Sherlock if he cheated on you?"

I paused for a moment, taken aback by Sophia's question. The thought of my husband being unfaithful made me feel physically sick. "To be honest, I don't know, Sophia. But I would at least question why before closing the door on everything we had built together."

I filled Sophia's glass with wine and sat quietly in the garden for a while. My heart went out to her. Our friendship had endured for over twenty years, since we were first-year students at La Scala. We loved spending time together. We'd forged a connection in those early days built on trust, fun, and a sense of similarity as we sought reflections of ourselves in each other. Sophia went home at three o'clock to prepare for her confrontation with Robert. She promised to let me know how it went. I sat in reflection for a while, finally realising I couldn't sit back and do nothing, I had to at least try to help my friend. I asked my coachman to take me to La Scala to confront Sophia's errant husband.

I found him alone in his office. Robert looked surprised to see me, but rose from his chair and kissed me, inviting me to sit beside his desk. "If you are here to lecture me, Nene, please don't bother. I couldn't possibly feel any worse than I do now. Sophia has asked me for a divorce and I'm at a loss as to what to do."

I stared at Robert. He looked to be on the verge of tears.

"You must fight for your wife and show her how much she means to you. Where is Mia now?"

"Gone, after I told her there was no future for us, even if Sophia divorced me. I pray to God she doesn't. I realised it was her and the children I love. I cannot believe that I have jeopardised our relationship, and for what? A meaningless fling." He scoffed. "Mia left yesterday to take up a position in Florence. We vowed never to see one another again." Robert was shaking, his eyes streaming with tears.

I reached into my bag and handed him a handkerchief, smiled at him sympathetically as he dabbed his eyes. "I saw Sophia earlier today. We had a luncheon together. I think it's fair to say that you have broken her heart. But Robert, it's not too late to make amends. Sophia told me she was prepared to talk to you when you arrive home this evening. So this is your one chance to redeem yourself and to put things right. For the sake of our friendship. and your relationship with Sophia and your children, please don't waste this opportunity, for I fear you will not get another."

Robert nodded. "Thank you, Nene. You've always been quite a friend to me and my wife. Is there anything else you think I should do?" He stared at me with a hopeful expression.

"Be honest with Sophia, and speak from the heart. I know she'll appreciate that. She will know if you lie to her." I smiled at him. "Also, flowers never go unappreciated. However, I think it best you do not mention I have been here today. Sophia would take a dim view of me meddling in her affairs. However, due to our history, I felt compelled to come and see you."

Robert and I embraced, and I wished him luck before I embarked on my journey home. I had just disembarked from the carriage and was making my way back into the house when a man I did not recognise, dressed in a hooded jacket, wellington boots, and gardening gloves — his silvery grey hair protruding from a battered Panama hat — appeared at the door.

I furrowed my brow. "May I help you?"

The man bowed, removing his hat and glasses. "I wondered if you required a gardener, Signora." he spoke in a thick Italian accent before bursting into uproarious laughter.

I shook my head and smiled. "Sherlock Holmes, you will be my death. What on earth have you been up to now?"

"Come inside," he said, taking my arm. "I will explain everything after a glass of whisky and a change of clothes."

I retired to the drawing room and poured my husband a whiskey and soda. When Sherlock came downstairs, changed into black trousers, a waistcoat, and a white shirt, he sipped from the glass. He explained he'd offered his services to Amato's housekeeper as a gardener and handyman after discovering the regular gardener had broken his leg in an accident. The housekeeper gladly accepted the offer of help. So my husband would be employed by the Amatos for the remainder of the week.

"Well, is this a lucrative sideline for when there is a lull in detective work?"

"Hmm, very funny, Mrs Sapori."

"It's exhausting being married to you sometimes. But why are you posing as a gardener at the Amatos? Are you not concerned that someone might discover who you are?"

"Not at all. If my wife failed to recognise me, then I think we can safely assume the Amatos will be impervious to my charms. Mr Amato has yet to meet me, and his wife barely glanced at me. She was too busy fussing over her husband."

"What exactly are you looking for?"

"Incriminating evidence. However, I will keep an open mind. After spending most of the afternoon at the property, I am familiar with the layout of the house. However, I may need to go back during the night hours. But, of course, my task would be much easier if only Watson were with me."

"I have no idea what you are expecting to find, but I would be willing to accompany you. In disguise, if needed."

Sherlock shook his head. "Thank you for the gesture, but I don't want to put you at risk. I expect to find all I need before the week's end. So come, let us prepare for dinner."

Chapter Eight: Revelations

The next few days passed without any undue drama. Instead, my husband snuck out of the house early each morning to resume his gardening duties at the Amatos' home. Never content with the moderate and the mundane, Sherlock was in his element, although I was convinced he was barking up the wrong tree. What on earth could the Amatos have to hide?

I remembered it was Wednesday when Renata called to see me. We took coffee in the garden, where she explained that her husband was feeling much better. He insisted that Lucca and I join them for dinner on Saturday. I gladly accepted the invitation. I knew Sherlock would be grateful for the opportunity to question Luigi.

When we dressed for dinner that night, I caught my husband's reflection in the pier glass as he fastened his shirt and donned his tie. "I hope this dinner will not be too taxing for you, Sherlock. Do you think you can cope with being your usual affable self?"

"Not unless you expect me to prove myself as some kind of lothario in front of your so-called friends."

I gasped in shock. "Could you be more patronising? But, of course, a husband is expected to support his wife. Would it hurt you to show some charm just for once?"

"You know I am no fan of social events. However, this deception is a necessary ploy to garner further information." He pulled on his jacket and headed towards the door, opening it. "Come. Our carriage awaits."

The hall clock struck eight as my husband and I entered the threshold of the Amato residence. Guilia escorted us to the lounge, where I introduced my husband to Luigi and Renata. The two men shook hands before we sat for pre-dinner drinks. Renata explained the Moons had politely declined the dinner invitation — of course, I knew the reason why.

Sherlock fixated on Luigi throughout our conversation, regarding our host with a rather piercing and steady state. Luigi was his usual charming self during dinner, although he looked a little gaunt. Since our last encounter, he had understandably lost weight. I asked him how he was, only for him to brush off my concerns with a dismissive wave of his hand.

"I am fine, Nene. It's good of you to ask. Although I would like to thank you for all you did for my wife. As far as Renata and I are concerned, you are a wonder to behold. We will be forever indebted to you."

"And I adore you for that." Renata smiled at me fondly.

I shook my head. "There is no need to thank me. Renata is my friend. I would do it all again in a moment."

Luigi turned his attention to my husband. "It is an honour to meet you, Signor Sapori. I have only heard good things about you. But, of course, I have already had the pleasure of meeting your beautiful, charming wife. That engaging smile could cast a spell over any man." He sighed. "You are, indeed, a fortunate man. Love is such a wonderful thing. Some say the most incredible thing. Don't you agree?"

Sherlock straightened in his chair. I could see this inference rattled him. "I'm afraid I don't speak as eloquently as you regarding matters of the heart, Signor Amato. Neither would I wish to. But I will say this." He paused to take a sip from his glass, fixing me with his piercing grey eyes. "My wife is not here to decorate the room, Signor Amato. She is a strong independent woman of whom I am inordinately proud. I admire many things about her, of course. Her grace, humility, and intelligence are just a few of the things that first attracted me to her. But, most of all, the fact that she chose me as her husband. Nene does not walk in my shadow. On the contrary, she ploughs her own furrow. I am a better person for knowing her."

My heart swelled as I stared at my husband in jaw-dropping incredulous admiration. It seemed unimaginable, this profound seismic moment. Sherlock's narrative, spoken so articulately, and hurtled so trippingly off the tongue and spoken with such certainty and conviction, was the last thing I expected to hear. Yet his words meant more to me than I could ever express.

"Come, let's have another drink." Luigi raised his glass. "A toast to the ladies — *in vino veritas.*"

After dinner, my husband and Luigi retired to the drawing room for brandy and cigars while Renata and I took coffee in the lounge. We chatted for a while, although my mind was distracted, wondering what Sherlock had discovered so far.

Renata told me that Luigi had been distant since he was discharged from the hospital. He appeared to have sunk into a deep depression, especially since she had told him the news of her father.

"That's understandable," I said. "Your husband has been through a lot recently. It's likely the medication is responsible for his mood change. He'll be fine, you'll see." I squeezed her arm reassuringly.

I felt relieved when Holmes and I finally left the Amatos. It was a lovely moonlight night, so we decided to walk home. I slipped my arm into his. "Sherlock, did you mean what you said at the Amato's?"

"Of course. I never have and will never lie to you."

"I thought you never got sentimental?"

"I don't, but why do you ask?" He chuckled.

"Because when you said those words at dinner, it was

probably the most memorable moment of my life. And you can never unsay it, husband."

"I have no wish to." He sighed. "I will never understand a woman like your friend, who appears to worship the ground Amato walks upon. Why, it's a mystery to me. Does she not realise how she wastes her life on a man like that? Choosing to listen to the meanderings of apathetic men instead of the unadulterated truth."

"What do you mean? What have you discovered?"

"I'm not sure who tried to murder Amato, but I know the man is a bounder and a feckless gambler and not a very good one."

"How do you know all this?"

"I enquired extensively at his club, the Casinò di Venezia. I struck up a conversation at the bar with one of the croupiers. After a few drinks, he revealed all he knew about Amato. He drew up a substantial line of credit with the club playing poker, a debt he has yet to repay."

"So he has money worries. But that doesn't make the man a bounder or a lothario."

"Ah, Nene. I noticed how he looked at you with more than friendly interest during dinner. You should always watch the eyes. They reveal what the soul is saying. There's a reason for all the subterfuge."

I stared at my husband with some surprise. I could see he was having trouble suppressing his rage.

"All right, if you say so. But Renata will be bereft if any of this comes to light. She adores Luigi."

"I'm aware of that. But your friend deserves to know the truth, although we shall keep our powder dry for now. I shall make further enquiries before we come to a definitive conclusion."

When we arrived home, we sat in the lounge, listening to Beethoven's *Fifth Symphony* on the gramophone.

Holmes smiled at me languidly as I kicked off my shoes. "Let's have a brandy, and then I suggest an early night. I have a long day ahead of me tomorrow."

"What on earth are you up to now?"

"My dearest Nene, apart from my gardening duties, tomorrow will find me auditioning with the Milano Theatre Company for the role of Macduff in the Scottish play, avenging the callous murder of my wife and children. I intend to attack the role with considerable aplomb."

"But isn't that Luigi's Company?"

"Indeed. So, I shall go in disguise. Although it's unlikely Amato will make an appearance. What do you think of my chances?"

"I think you could play all the parts, even the witches. You are a fine actor, for sure."

He handed me a glass of brandy. "Thank you, my dear, you are too kind. Come, let's take our drinks to bed."

Chapter Nine: Forgiveness and Fortitude

I met Sophia for lunch at Emilio's restaurant in the old town the following afternoon. Sophia revealed she'd had a heart-to-heart with Robert and persuaded him to visit his physician, Doctor Accardi. After a thorough examination, Accardi reassured Robert that he did not have Parkinson's. Instead, the doctor said Robert's hand tremors resulted from his heavy drinking and cocaine misuse, along with the stress, grief, and anxiety brought on by his father's death. Accardi recommended a specialised diet, rest, and relaxation to alleviate Robert's melancholy. As a result, Robert swore to stop taking cocaine and cut down on the drink.

Sophia revealed her husband broke down in tears and begged for forgiveness, explaining his erratic behaviour was because he expected to die like his father before him. Robert's assistant Mia had already left her position and he swore she meant nothing to him. It was just a fling, which he was profoundly ashamed of and deeply regretted. After talking for hours, Sophia had finally agreed to give Robert another chance. However, she warned her husband if it ever happened again, she would not hesitate to file for a divorce.

I squeezed Sophia's hand. "I am so glad that you and Robert have decided to reconcile. I know from personal experience that grief can do the strangest things to people. It can skew thoughts for a while, but unfortunately, grief is something one never gets over. Instead, you must find a way to swerve around the heartache."

Sophia nodded. "Yes, and I must take some of the blame. I have neglected Robert, I can see that now. I have been so busy with rehearsals and the children, I failed to see that he was suffering. Robert and I have been together too long to throw everything away. So we've decided to make more time for each other. We plan to take the children and holiday in Venice at the beginning of August. Admittedly, things are still rather strained between us, but I'm sure we will eventually resolve matters. I can't believe I'm saying this, but I suppose we have your husband to thank for spotting the warning signs."

"Well, he is a celebrated detective." We laughed.

Sophia excused herself to retire to the lady's bathroom. I took a sip from my glass, gazing out the window, watching the world go by. I spotted Renata's maid, Giulia, embarking from the cafe across the road, chatting and laughing gaily on the arm of a young man. I was not aware she had a sweetheart. I smiled, thinking she looked happy and rather fetching in a black frock coat and a black plumed hat. But my smile was quickly eradicated when I looked down and noticed she was wearing four-inch red heels.

I explained my concerns to Sherlock later that night over dinner.

"But lots of women wear heels," he argued, appearing unconcerned with my findings.

"Yes, of course, they do," I agreed. "But, even though it was Giulia's day off, it's most unusual for a maid to be seen wearing heels during the day."

"Don't worry, I am making excellent headway with my inquiries. The trap is almost set."

"Whatever do you mean?"

Sherlock kissed me lightly on the head as he rose from his chair. "All will be revealed soon, you'll see. Do you have any plans for tomorrow evening, Nene?"

"Nothing pressing."

"Excellent, please keep the night free. I intend to break into the Amato's, and I would like you to come with me as my accomplice. Albeit in disguise, of course."

I stared at him incredulously. "But why the sudden change of heart?"

"Ah, with Watson not here to assist me, you must become my accomplice."

"Well, I certainly have some big shoes to fill. I hope I can do the good doctor justice. But why tomorrow night?"

"It's the servant's day off, and the maid Giulia confided that she's going into town to meet her sweetheart. I discovered the Amatos retire early, around nine o'clock. They both take sleeping drafts, so we should have a clear run if we can get there around nine-thirty. I will unlock the side gate before I leave tomorrow afternoon. The Amatos keep a spare back door key under a plant pot in the garden."

I shook my head, gazing at my husband in admiration. "Sherlock, what you do is incredible. I would consider it an honour and a privilege to accompany you."

So just after nine o'clock the following night, my husband and I took a cab to the Amato residence in disguise—me in a gingham skirt and jacket and a fetching blonde wig which I tied up in a ponytail, and Sherlock in a black sack suit and billycock with a red wig and thick horn-rimmed glasses. We looked every inch like a commonplace courting couple.

We asked the coachman to stop two streets away from the Amato residence and walked the rest. We approached the villa at twilight, slipping quietly around the back. The side door was ajar, as my husband had left it. Sherlock quickly retrieved the key, using his torch to identify the flowerpot. We entered the house quietly, the only noise a bat screeching in the distance. We entered Luigi's study. Sherlock quietly rifled through the desks and drawers, finding only a stack of unpaid bills and a letter addressed to the theatre company from the bailiff, along with an antique pocket watch with the initials LE engraved on the back. Sherlock whispered that it was safe and gestured for me to go upstairs while he checked out the lounge. I made my way to the second floor, to Giulia's room, which my husband told me was the third room on the right. I was relieved to find it open, although the door creaked on its hinges. I hesitated for a moment, hoping I hadn't disturbed the Amatos, my heart pounding.

Then I realised I was excited by this adrenaline rush, and I got a glimpse of why my husband loved his work so passionately. The room's neatness struck me as odd — beautifully decorated with floral wallpaper and borders, a matching bedspread and curtains. The carpet was a luxurious deep pile twist, and a taper candle flickered in the corner next to a neatly made single bed with a mahogany headboard and matching wardrobe and chest of drawers. I opened the cabinet, which contained nothing unusual, apart from a red feather Bauer hat. Next I opened the drawers containing underwear, clothes, hats, scarves, and gloves. Finally, I took out the torch Sherlock had given me and shone it under the bed. And that was when I discovered a staggering assortment of shoes and boots, all different sizes, including a pair of well-worn red heels size four, sitting next to a pair of pink satin slippers.

I checked the dressing table covered with various items of makeup consisting of rouges, face powders, lip dyes, and tinctures, along with several bottles of French perfumes, most notably a bottle of Marie Farnina's eau de cologne. I raised my eyebrows as I knew that was expensive. Sherlock had bought me a bottle for my birthday. I figured Renata must pay her staff well. Next my eyes were drawn to a jewellery casket. I opened it and peered inside, staggered by the delicate pieces, necklaces, dress rings, bracelets, and strings of pearls. I wondered how Giulia could afford such things on a maid's wage, unless they belonged to her late mother. At least that was plausible and the only reasonable explanation, as far as I was concerned. Next, I picked up a bottle of eye drops. I opened it carefully and recognised the smell of nightshade from the belladonna plant. Many women used these drops out of vanity, and to follow social trends to create a light effect and dilate their pupils. Even so, I was aware from what Sherlock told me that belladonna could cause blindness if used for long periods. Some women took it even further to maintain the pale-skinned pallor they craved, using ammonia to wash their faces. But why would a commonplace housemaid have all these things and go to all that trouble? It didn't make any sense.

I was about to slip downstairs when I heard a knock at the front door. I took a breath, terrified of being discovered. I listened as a bedroom door opened on the floor below and footsteps walked down the stairs. Finally, I stood on the landing only to hear a muffled voice speaking in the inner hallway. I took off my shoes and tentatively tiptoed downstairs, hoping Sherlock had heard the commotion. As I got to the bottom of the second set of stairs, I could hear Luigi speaking to someone, his tone sharp and decisive.

"I told you not to come here. Renata isn't stupid," he hissed. "The last thing we need is for her to become suspicious." Another male voice responded, but it was difficult to determine what he was saying. Luigi paused for a moment. "Yes, I know it's all a mess. I don't need you to tell me that. I need time to think before we decide what to do next. You need to go. We shall speak tomorrow."

I slipped into the parlour and hid behind the door. I dared not move. Sweating profusely, I hardly dared to breathe until

I heard the bedroom door close. Then I slowly made my way out through the conservatory, my heart pounding uncontrollably in my chest. I heard the sound of shuffling feet behind me, and I turned around, relieved to find my husband following me out into the garden.

"Are you all right, Nene," he whispered. "Forgive me, I shouldn't have brought you here. I would never forgive myself if anything happened to you."

I shook my head. "No, I am fine. I quite enjoyed it. I appear to have a taste for it now. But don't even try to talk me out of doing it again."

Sherlock feigned horror at my suggestion before bursting into quiet laughter. "My darling, that's the spirit that will take you wherever you want to go. But, as rousing as this is, we must leave at once."

We looked upwards as the light of a taper candle flickered in the bedroom window and Renata's lap dog Tiggi barked in the distance. I watched anxiously as my husband locked the back door, replacing the key under the flowerpot before we went out via the side gate. With no cabs in sight, we walked home, my arm in his, continually looking over my shoulder, wondering if anyone was following us.

When we arrived at the villa, I sat down on the chaise lounge, removed my wig and shoes. Sherlock poured out a brandy, which I gratefully sipped as I relayed all I had found in Giulia's room.

"What about the clandestine conversation? Did you hear that?" I asked.

"Yes, indeed. And from his dulcet tones, I think I may know the perpetrator's identity."

"It appears obvious that Luigi is up to something. Although for Renata's sake, I pray to God that we are wrong. But it's the red shoes and the red feather Bauer hat that intrigues me the most, Giulia was not the girl I saw in the lane."

Holmes smiled grimly. "There is more to this case than meets the eye. There are so many inconsistencies and layers to unfold. We need more data. It is a capital mistake to theorise without it. But tomorrow may find us the last piece in the puzzle."

"And how will we do that?"

"Why tomorrow, we shall visit Milo Endrizzi at the Policlinico hospital."

CHAPTER TEN: THE CONFESSIONS OF MILO ENDRIZZI

Sherlock and I arrived at the Policlinico hospital just after luncheon the following day. A nurse ushered us towards the second room on the left, in a private ward.

We tentatively entered the room to find Milo Endrizzi on the bed, propped up by pillows, his yellow-tinged skin stretched like old parchment over his cheeks. Large brown eyes protruding from his shaven head stared at us behind a pair of thick-rimmed glasses, following us around the room. I took a breath, taking in his emaciated appearance. Milo was only in his late thirties, but he looked like an old man. Nevertheless, he smiled when he saw us approach and listened attentively as Sherlock patiently explained that we had come on behalf of Renata and her father.

Milo half lifted his head from the pillow, and a glimmer of a smile appeared on his lips. "Forgive me, Signor Sapori" — he gestured to his glasses — "My sight is poor. How can you expect me to trust you when I can hardly see you and don't even know who you are?"

Milo motioned to the pitcher of water on his bedside locker. I poured out a glass and handed it to him. "Thank you," he said. "Forgive me if I appear curt. But I don't receive many visitors. I suspect your visit has to do with Lorenzo Rossi's release from prison after my testimony to the authorities." He grimaced. "The irony is the Polizia would have arrested me for subverting the course of justice if I wasn't already on my deathbed. Some might describe it as poetic justice, me terminally ill with leukaemia, and they would be right. But I deserve to die after what I did to that wretched man. I am finally paying the price."

"It wasn't your fault!" I exclaimed. "You were a child, badly let down by the one person responsible for protecting you."

Milo nodded. "Yes, I realise that now. The Polizia assure me they are doing all they can to have my father deported from Australia. They have issued an extradition order. However, he is proving a slippery fish to catch."

"Don't worry," said Sherlock. "I have excellent contacts with the British Government. They will eventually track your father down. You have my word on that."

"Thank you. That is of some comfort at least." Milo opened the drawer next to his bedside and pulled out a large brown envelope and handed it to my husband. "Would you please ensure Signor Rossi gets this? It is a copy of my last will, including a letter of apology. My lawyers have the original documents. The contact details are within the letter. I never married or had any children. After what happened to me, I found holding down any meaningful relationships impossible. You see, we had a difficult childhood, my siblings and me. We were all affected by our mother's controlling behaviour. She had a cold and manipulative nature. Your mother is the one person who is supposed to nurture you and offer unconditional love, the only kind that truly matters. Instead, we were lost, vulnerable, and unloved children. There was no happy ending."

He sighed. "My brother and sister couldn't wait to leave home. However, my sister was fortunate — she married well. As for my brother, from what I hear, he has done all right for himself. My family does not need my help, although I would love to see them again before I die to explain what happened.

Still, they would be shocked to see me like this, the shadow of the man I used to be." He grimaced. "So I decided to leave everything I own to Mr Rossi, as I believe it is the right thing to do. After my brother died, I spent hours being questioned by the Polizia. I remember my father saying *Tell the officer what Rossi did, then you can go home.* Every night, I see that poor man's face in my dreams, screaming as he is dragged from the dock by the guards. I remember his final words. *Ask the boy,* he cried. He knows the truth! For years I begged my father to go to the authorities and confess what happened. He refused. He said if we did, we would all go to prison, and my brother and sister would end up in the orphanage. Or worse still, the workhouse. And I knew I couldn't allow that to happen. Someone had to look after the children. My father wasn't fit for that purpose. And as for my mother, it was obvious she was mentally ill. She began to see things and hear voices. The irony is that she was ignored when she tried to confess to what she had done, finally overwhelmed by grief and remorse. People considered her deranged."

"So your father pressured you into lying?" quizzed Sherlock.

Milo nodded. "Yes, that's right. I knew it was wrong, but my family had suffered enough. So when my mother's life ended in the asylum, I decided to come forward. My brother Pedro could be a handful at times. He often cheeked up to our parents. And, of course, my brother paid for his cheek with his life."

A tear ran down Milo's face. I topped up his glass with water and handed him a handkerchief.

Milo sighed deeply, wiping the corner of his eye, before continuing. "So I left Rossi my villa in Bergamo, where I also own a small hotel, The Grand, and it's doing well. So at least this way Rossi will be financially secure. I hope he will eventually find it in his heart to forgive me."

Milo hesitated momentarily, taking a sip of water. "At least I can go to my maker knowing I have done everything possible to atone for my behaviour. I believe it was Harriet Beecher Stowe who said *The bitterest tears shed over graves are for words left unsaid and deeds left undone.* How fitting are those words" He sighed. "I'm not afraid to die. You see, I can no longer bear the pain." He closed his eyes and lay his head back on the pillow. "Forgive me, for I am exhausted and I need to rest."

Sherlock and I stood, as though ready to go, but instead, I squeezed Milo's hand and kissed him gently on the cheek. Finally, I whispered, "God have mercy on your soul." I wiped away a tear. Again, you could feel a sense of emptiness in the room. It was difficult to shake off that haunted look in his eyes. The acceptance of impending death clouded his face with a serenity that shocked and humbled me simultaneously. Then as we reached the door, my husband turned around and asked the question I had been expecting to hear since we entered the room in the sure knowledge that he already knew the answer.

"I realise you no longer see your brother and sister, Signor Endrizzi, and I'm sorry, I wish I could do something about that. But pray to tell me, what are the names of your siblings'?"

Milo's eyes glazed over, then, he flashed a wry smile. "Oh, how I would love to see my brother and sister one last time, but alas, that's not meant to be. My beautiful sister is called Olivia and my brother was named Ludwig after my grandfather—he inherited his talent for music. How I miss his precious laugh. However, Ludwig was always affectionately known to his friends and family as Luigi."

Chapter Eleven: Malice Afore-thought

I awoke early the following morning, but not before Sherlock, who had a breakfast meeting in the old town with inspector Romano. I decided to visit Milo at the hospital. But first I would make a detour into town to pick up a few items from the shopping mall, including pyjamas, underwear, and fresh fruit. It was the servants' half day, so I put a chicken in the oven before I embarked on my journey, as I was expecting my husband to join me later for dinner.

I was about to get into my carriage when I saw Giulia coming up the drive on a bicycle. She looked as though she had been crying. Acknowledging my presence, she stopped to talk to me.

"Are you alright?" I asked.

"Yes, I'm fine. I'm worried about my mistress and her husband. Do you think Signor Amato is going to be all right?"

I smiled at the girl and gently squeezed her hand. "I'm sure of it. He has the best doctors taking good care of him and they expect a full recovery."

"Good, I'm glad. My mistress would be distraught if anything happened to him." She stared at me imploringly. "Please don't tell Signora Amato that I said anything, I have no wish for her to be concerned. She has enough to deal with. I realise I'm being selfish, but I don't know what I would do if anything happened to her. There is no one else, you see."

"It's fine, Giulia, your secret is safe. Renata told me what happened and the special connection you forged after the train crash that cruelly ended your parents' lives. So I understand. Please do not hesitate to come and see me if you have any other concerns. My door is always open."

Giulia smiled, an expression of the utmost gratitude and relief on her face. She said she would be humbled to do so and thanked me for my kindness. I wished her a good morning, watching for a moment as she turned the bicycle around and pedalled down the drive. I continued my journey into town, finally arriving at the Policlinico Hospital.

As I approached the nurse's station and introduced myself, the matron acknowledged me as I made my way toward the entrance to the ward. "Signor Endrizzi will be delighted to see you, Signora Sapori. Your visit will help brighten his mood. You are his second visitor today."

Milo appeared pleased to see me. He seemed genuinely touched by my humble gifts. I gestured to the fresh-cut flowers on his bedside locker. "I believe you had another visitor earlier today," I gently quizzed, smiling at him curiously.

Milo nodded. "Yes, my brother discovered I was here. I never realised he lived in Milan. So I got quite a surprise. Although I barely recognised him. He's changed much since we were boys. He didn't stay long, but at least I have made peace with him. My brother forgave me."

"Does he plan to visit you again?"

"No, I asked him not to. I think it's for the best. Although there was one thing I found strange."

"And what was that?"

"His laugh... it was different."

I arrived home to a burning smell wafting in from the direction of the kitchen. I quickly turned off the oven, covering my face with a towel before opening the window to eliminate the billowing smoke. I placed the offending chicken on the kitchen table. The poor fowl was as black as coal.

I heard a sound and turned around to find Sherlock standing in the doorway. He looked at me with an amused expression. "What is that?" He cast his eyes over my burnt offerings.

"I think it's best we eat out this evening."

We arrived at Lafayette at eight o'clock. I glanced across the restaurant and noticed my old friend Lucrezia at dinner with her husband, Ferrando. I went over to speak to them briefly, congratulating them on the recent birth of their daughter Amara. When I returned to the table, the sommelier had already poured the wine.

"I've ordered," said Sherlock, flippantly gesturing towards the menu.

"Of course you have. Let me guess, fish for me and mutton for you?"

"Hmm, I'll make a good detective out of you yet."

We discussed our findings over dinner. My husband did not appear surprised when I told him Luigi had made an appearance at the hospital. Instead, he stared at me intensely as I relayed Milo's comments about his brother.

"This case gets stranger by the second." He sighed. I could sense Sherlock's frustration.

"You never told me what happened when you went to Luigi's theatre Company for your audition."

"Ah, that. Well, I was naturally magnificent, of course. But not good enough to land the part. When Amato's business partner, Edoardo Bruni, offered me the understudy position, I was somewhat flattered. I agreed, of course, so as not to alert suspicion. But the next day I messaged and made excuses, politely turning down the role, which was a shame as I would love to have acted alongside Bruni's sister, an actress of the highest calibre. Her portrayal of Lady Macbeth was beguiling."

"Did you discover anything else of interest while you were there?"

"From what I observed, the company seemed a decent bunch, as most actors are. Apart from Edoardo Bruni. There was something off about him that struck me as peculiar."

"Do you think he's in cahoots with Luigi?"

"I think they are thick as thieves," he said gravely. "I overheard him tell one of the cast members that he would be at dinner with the Amatos this Saturday. Finally, things are beginning to make sense." Sherlock took my hand and gazed at me solemnly. "When we arrive home, I want you to send a message with the coachman to the Amatos inviting them to dinner this coming Saturday."

I stared at my husband, shaking my head in disbelief. "Let me get this right. You want me to invite the Amatos for dinner? Mr and Mrs Sapori are to entertain?" I laughed out loud at the absurdity of the statement. That would be the last thing I thought my husband would ever ask me to do.

Sherlock shook his head. "I don't for one moment expect them to accept. Perish the thought. But I know the Moons are going to this little gathering. So that being the case, I hope the Amatos will feel compelled to extend the invitation to the Saporis."

I furrowed my brow. "Hmm, I wonder why the Amatos did not invite us in the first place. Still, they understand Lucca Sapori is no fan of social events. You play havoc with my social life, husband."

"Very droll."

When we arrived home, I duly obliged and wrote a note to Renata, and our coachman delivered it that evening. The following day Renata called to see me shortly after breakfast.

"Darling, I am so glad you got in touch. I was about to message you," she gushed. "Luigi and I are hosting an intimate dinner party this Saturday, Luigi's business partner and Robert and Sophia Moon. Luigi and I would be delighted if you and your husband would join us. If Lucca cannot make it, then come on your own."

"That's very kind of you, but, on the contrary, my husband and I would be thrilled to join you. We would consider it an honour."

"Well, that's settled then. Luigi and I shall look forward to seeing you both." I offered Renata coffee, but she refused my invitation. "I must get back to my husband. I need to ensure he's taking his medication." She kissed me fondly before dashing out to her carriage.

I entered the parlour to inform my husband his idea had worked. He smiled and poured me a cup of caffé noir while listening to Richard Wagner. I sipped from my cup, pondering how the dinner party would play out. I was bemused by the fact that it would be the first time Sophia and Sherlock would be in a room together since their confrontation. From what Sophia had told me, things were still somewhat strained between her and Robert. And as for Sherlock and Luigi, one could hardly describe them as the best of friends. Nevertheless, I felt relieved it was not me hosting the dinner party. I wasn't expecting it to be the most congenial of atmospheres.

CHAPTER TWELVE: THE CONFRONTATION

"You have to admit that Luigi and Renata have a splendid home," I remarked to my husband as our carriage pulled up outside the Amatos' villa on Saturday evening.

"I suppose it has a certain colonial charm," he begrudgingly replied, casting his piercing eyes over the building.

We soon found ourselves in the drawing room of the Amato residence for a pre-dinner drinks reception. Sherlock and I were the last to arrive, so after introductions we were ushered to the Chesterfield settee by Giulia, who deftly returned with our drinks, a whiskey and soda for my husband and a glass of dry sherry for me. I glanced at Sophia and Robert. Sitting together on the chaise lounge, they appeared united on the face of it. But their facial expressions spoke volumes, and they were barely speaking. I hoped this wouldn't set the tone for the remainder of the evening.

On the other hand, Luigi's business partner Edoardo Bruni was the party's life and soul. Tall and slim, with jet-black hair and intense brown eyes, and with a very engaging manner, albeit he came across as a little pompous. Nevertheless, he entertained us with anecdotes from his life as an actor. I noticed Sherlock raising an eyebrow as the narrative continued far too long for his liking. However, Renata and Sophia enjoyed Bruni's stories, laughing in all the appropriate places. I noticed Luigi was quieter than usual, as though the weight of the world was on his shoulders.

After Giulia cleared the dessert plates and our glasses were topped up with wine, the evening suddenly turned sinister. The door to the dining room flew open. A woman of considerable — if haughty — beauty dramatically swept into the room. She was tall and slim, dressed in a black silk dress with lace sleeves and a black felt hat with a slanted brim. Her piercing brown eyes flashed with fire as she averted her gaze to Luigi.

The woman was quickly followed into the room by a flustered-looking Giulia. "I'm sorry," she stammered. "But the lady barged past me."

"It's all right." Renata smiled sympathetically at the girl. "Go back into the kitchen and have some tea. You haven't done anything wrong."

The blood had drained from Luigi's face as he sat motionless, his lips pressed tight. Observing his startled expression, the woman gave a throaty laugh. All eyes were fixed on her as she held the room's attention. "What's the matter, brother? Weren't you expecting me? Why, my invitation must have gotten lost in the post." She laughed derisively before turning her attention to the rest of her captive audience. "Forgive me, I'm afraid I have taken a terrible liberty. But please allow me to introduce myself, as my brother appears a little tongue-tied. My name is Olivia Conte, nee Endrizzi." She arched an eyebrow. "You still don't get the connection?" She drew closer to Luigi with an intense expression. "Please allow me to enlighten you. My brother changed his surname by deed poll while he was a student, for professional reasons. Unfortunately, there was already another actor named Luigi Endrizzi."

Sherlock pulled out a chair, gesturing for Olivia to join us around the dining table. He poured out a glass of wine and handed it to her. She sipped from it, giving Sherlock a cursory nod before turning her attention back to her brother. "Why didn't you tell me about Milo? Am I to be the last person to know that my brother is dying?"

Luigi glanced across at his sister. "Milo didn't want you to know. I only found out recently that he was in the Policlinico hospital after an anonymous tip-off. Our brother would like to die in peace. So I don't understand why you are here, sister."

Olivia shook her head. "I also saw Milo this morning after receiving a telegram from a well-wisher revealing his illness and your address, Luigi. Our brother told me the shocking truth, everything that occurred between Pedro and our mother. Milo said that when you visited him, he barely recognised you."

I stared at Sherlock, who smiled at me pensively, and I instinctively knew my husband was the anonymous tipster. "Well, he wouldn't, would he?" Interrupted Sherlock, diverting his gaze to Luigi. "For you were never at the hospital, Amato. Rather it was your friend, Signor Bruni, who visited your dying brother — posing as you. Your brother's eyesight has always been poor. As you know, he wore glasses from childhood. So when Bruni called on him, your brother failed to recognise him. But his laugh gave it away, as your brother explained to my wife when she saw him only yesterday."

Renata gasped. "Luigi, please tell us this is not true! What else have you kept from me?"

Luigi shook his head. "I couldn't go to see Milo. It would have been too much after all that had transpired when we were children. But I didn't want him to think I didn't care. So Edoardo agreed to cover for me."

"Yes," said Sherlock. "But that is not the real reason you refused to visit your brother. However I will get to that. For it is your most recent activities that intrigued me the most. If your mind appears hazy, Amato, please let me remind you of the events leading up to this shocking crime. First, I know all about your failing business and gambling debts. Your outrageous attempt to frame your wife, the woman you vowed to love and protect, for a crime she did not commit. Your lust for money, one of the oldest motives known to man, led to this traitorous defection." Sherlock glared at Luigi. "With your wife languishing in jail for attempted murder, you alone would have access to her estate. You needed the money to pay off your debts and save your theatre company."

"My, you have been busy," sneered Luigi, staring at Holmes with a hateful stare. "We are all men of the world, Sapori."

"This is not a game, Amato! I would hate to live in your world. Why, you and your accomplice are nothing more than petty crooks," replied Sherlock.

Renata was sobbing uncontrollably, rendered speechless by my husband's shocking narrative. Sophia had her arm around her friend, holding her tightly in an act of empathy and comfort.

"And I'll tell you something else," said Sherlock, regarding Luigi with some disdain. "The incident at the insurance company. The woman who posed as your wife was your colleague and fellow actress from the Milano Theatre Company, Nadia Bruni, an actress of remarkable ability. Along with the assistance of belladonna eye drops that my wife reliably informs me are often used to enhance ladies' pupils, and strategically placed make-up and wig use, Signora Bruni set the scene to foil the insurance company. And, of course, she left the gloves deliberately, knowing the clerk would run after her and discover her imaginary lover. Amato, the accomplice and the man who impersonated you so admirably at the hospital yesterday, are one and the same. Signora Bruni's brother, your friend, and colleague, the actor Edoardo Bruni."

"How could you possibly know any of this?" exclaimed Bruni.

"Shut up, Edoardo," snarled Luigi. "You fool, don't you see you are playing into his hands?"

My husband smiled sardonically. "Why, I am surprised you don't remember me. Only recently did you offer me the position of understudy in the Scottish play, although I was in disguise, of course. I overheard you and your sister in the dressing room, discussing your recent impromptu roles posing as lovers, from your sister's narrative. It was obvious she was under the impression your deception was nothing more than a practical joke. It was clear to me that Signora Bruni is not the vindictive type, unlike her brother. You and Amato have all the morals of an alley cat. But then I realised this practical joke was something far more sinister. It hardly took a genius to come to the correct conclusion. Although I have to say, your sister's interpretation of Lady Macbeth was mesmerising. She is indeed an accomplished actress."

"No, no, this cannot be happening," sobbed Renata, diverting her gaze to Luigi. "You married me for my money? How dare you? I believe I am going insane!"

"You are not insane," said Sherlock. "Although perhaps a little misguided."

Luigi remained silent, casting his eyes downwards.

"It wasn't only the money," Sherlock continued gravely, directing his gaze on Renata. "I'm afraid your fate was sealed when you revealed your identity. You unwittingly stepped straight into the lion's den. For it was also out of exact and intimate revenge that Amato set his cap at you. You see, he held your father responsible for his brother's death and his family's subsequent fragmentation."

"But, Luigi, you knew my father didn't kill your brother," cried Renata.

Luigi nodded. "I know that now, but not at the time. Milo and my father convinced me it was Rossi, and the courts convicted him of murder, and then I met you, Renata." Luigi shrugged. "So when you told me what happened with your father and adoptive parents, I thought why should you benefit from my brother's death? So I put my plans into action. The hard part was trying to get you to fall for me."

Renata stared at Luigi, tears streaming down her face. "You bastard," she said. "How could you? I loved you. I thought we would have children and grow old together."

Olivia laughed, staring incredibly at Renata. "But Luigi is already married, my dear, to his childhood sweetheart, Melissa." She glared at her brother. "You abandoned the poor girl when you grew tired of her. Discarded her like a broken toy. However, Melissa couldn't afford to divorce you. She naively hoped you might return one day."

"Hold your tongue, woman," cried Luigi, staring daggers at his sister. "Despite what you think, I loved Melissa." Luigi turned to his wife. "Like I learned to love you, Renata. When you came to the hospital, I realised how much you cared for me. And for what it's worth, I am truly sorry."

"You don't even know the meaning of the word," snarled Renata. "But I don't understand why you faked the poisoning. I find it unfathomable. You could have died, for god's sake."

Luigi cast his eyes down. "Admittedly, I miscalculated the dosage. But, you see, I was a desperate man. I eavesdropped on some of your private conversations with Robert Moon, then witnessed your easy familiarity with each other at La Scala. There was a rumour circulating the opera house that Moon was having an extramarital affair, and I became convinced it was with you, Renata. I was terrified you were about to leave me and that would have ruined everything you see."

"So you put two and two together and got five!" exclaimed Renata. "There has never been anything going on between Robert and me. He and Sophia have been so kind to me during my time at La Scala. Sophia is like Nene, one of my closest confidantes. I would never do anything to disrespect either of them. The last laugh is on you, Luigi, because there never was any inheritance. At least not for me."

Luigi looked at her, appalled. "What's that supposed to mean?"

Renata shook her head, staring at Luigi in disbelief. Sophia and Robert sat in stunned solemn silence, their expressions frozen in awe and amazement by the narrative, which was fascinating and petrifying in equal measure. However, I noticed Robert slip his hand into Sophia's and squeeze, and he threw his arm around her shoulder protectively. She responded by offering him a weak smile. Perhaps she realised her philandering husband wasn't so bad after Luigi's antics. I figured Robert was a choir boy in comparison.

My husband turned his attention to Luigi. "And then we come back to your brother's death, and the real reason you refused to visit him in the hospital. Don't be coy. Pray, tell us what it was."

"I thought you had all the answers, Sapori. Who do you think you are? Sherlock Holmes?"

My husband sighed. "I am flattered by the comparison to the celebrated detective, but I work for his brother. It was an unimaginably stupid act, Amato, sending someone to the hospital to pose as you. But I believe I know why. Something happened that morning between your brother Pedro and you. What was it?"

Luigi shook his head, casting his eyes downwards. "Yes, you're right. And I've carried the burden ever since. Pedro had entered my bedroom earlier that morning after we had a petty disagreement. I can't even remember why. However, Pedro trashed the room and broke my violin in the process. That was my pride and joy, the last gift from my grandfather before he died. And I discovered the engraved pocket watch he'd also gifted me discarded on the floor, the glass shattered.

I was heartbroken, and then I became angry at the disrespect. But when I confronted Pedro, he mocked me and refused to apologise. I vowed to find a way to punish him. I was in the garden later that morning when the incident occurred with our mother. I saw her chasing him. Pedro was laughing, as he knew he could outrun her. But I figured he deserved a beating. So as Pedro passed me, I tripped him up. My brother fell to the ground, hitting his head on a rock. I noticed the blood, and I thought I'd knocked him out. But then he opened his eyes and smirked at me. Seeing my mother approach, I ran back into the house. I had no idea what was about to happen." Luigi paused for a moment, half-closing his eyes. "I was so busy worrying about what I had done that I failed to notice the poker." Luigi sighed. "So, I am as responsible as my mother for Pedro's death. He would probably still be alive if it weren't for me."

"What happened to your brother, what you did, was a tragic accident, I'll grant you that. But what you are guilty of is what you tried to do to a young vulnerable woman. At your core is someone quite malevolent, for it took a cunning mind and a cold heart to execute this dastardly plan."

Luigi narrowed his eyes. "You think you are so clever, Sapori. But let me be clear, you and Renata have robbed me of everything. It's all gone, ruined. The two of you are responsible for the broken dreams and my profound despondency. So you see, I have nothing left to lose." Luigi stared at Sherlock menacingly. Reaching into his pocket, he pulled out a gun as the final thread holding back his heinous wickedness finally gave way. But my husband had already pulled out a pistol as he stood and advanced toward the two men.

"Put it down, Sapori, or I'll shoot the women, starting with your lovely wife."

Sherlock stopped in his tracks, manoeuvring his body between Luigi and the women before slowly placing the revolver on the dining table. Luigi gestured for him to take a step back.

"Edoardo, check if Signora Sapori has a weapon," he cried.

"Only my infectious smile," I quipped in a desperate effort to defuse the situation, although I was shaking inside, my heart beating uncontrollably.

"You're despicable cowards. Lay one finger on these women and I will finish you," Sherlock exclaimed, diverting his thunderous gaze to Edoardo Bruni.

Edoardo shook his head as a cry of despair escaped his mouth. "You go too far, Amato. After the insurance company's deception, you told me we would all be rich. I cannot be involved in anything like this. I have a reputation to uphold."

"A reputation that's now in tatters," I exclaimed. "Why is it always the men with dirty hands who point the finger?"

"Give it up," said Sherlock. "Put the gun away, Amato. This building is surrounded. You don't stand a chance."

Olivia, who had sat in stunned silence during this time, dove forward and grabbed Sherlock's revolver, pointing it straight at her brother. "Put it down, Luigi. Don't you think you have done enough damage?"

"Olivia, don't force me to shoot you," screamed Luigi.

I gasped, stunned not only by Luigi's actions but the ferocity of his words. Tears were flowing down Olivia's face as she made to pull back the trigger.

"Don't do it," cried Sherlock "This man is not worth spending the rest of your life in prison."

Before Olivia had time to answer, the dining room door burst open. Inspector Romano and three constables, all armed with guns, flooded the room as their eyes scoured the scene. Olivia placed the revolver carefully on the table. Luigi tried to make a run for it, but Sherlock hit him with a blow to the chin, which sent Luigi reeling onto the floor.

"That's for my wife and the other women." Sherlock stared at Luigi contemptuously as the constables dragged him onto his feet.

At the same time, Romano arrested Luigi Amato and his accomplice, Edoardo Bruni. Romano read out the countless charges, which included subverting the course of justice, providing false testimony to prove an innocent person guilty, incriminating an innocent person, and finally, using a firearm in a threatening manner likely to cause injury or death.

As he was led away in handcuffs, I felt almost sorry for Luigi Amato. He had been very clever, but not quite clever enough. He had not expected to come across the brilliant mind of the world's finest consulting detective, albeit in disguise.

Sherlock nodded to Romano, gesturing towards his two prisoners. "Inspector, please remove this odious pair from our sight."

A long, intense drama had reached its climax, like the final movement of a great concerto, its conductor, the most celebrated detective of his time, Sherlock Holmes. When Romano, his constables and the two perpetrators finally left, we all sat stunned.

"I think what everyone needs now is a stiff drink," said Sherlock.

Renata rang the bell and asked Giulia to bring brandy, which we all gratefully sipped. Robert organised a hansom to take a stunned Olivia back to her hotel. I sat on the chaise lounge with Renata and put my arm around her.

"Don't cry, or you will start me crying," I said to Renata, before glancing over at my husband. "Now?" I mouthed. He nodded.

"Renata, my husband would like to speak to your maid. Could you please send for her?" Renata looked at me oddly but did as I asked, deftly sounding the bell. A somewhat puzzled Giulia entered the room, staring at us anxiously.

Holmes asked Giulia to take a seat. He handed her a small glass of brandy. I sat down next to her, taking her hand in mine.

"Don't be alarmed, you are not in any trouble," I said. "My husband would like to ask you a few questions."

Renata furrowed her brow. "What are you doing?" she quizzed. "Giulia is not involved in this dreadful business. She could do nothing wrong."

"Yes, we know that, but two deceptions are going on here," said Sherlock. He turned his attention to Giulia and gently stroked the hair back from her face. "Forgive me," he said as he uncovered a strawberry birthmark under her hairline. Renata and I gasped in shock while Sophia looked on in bemusement.

Sherlock indicated with a tilt of his head, staring at the maid. "Will the real Renata please reveal herself?" We all stared in astonishment as Giulia, encouraged by Renata, slowly removed her thick black glasses and a red wig, revealing a mop of lustrous dark hair. But then there was a collective gasp of surprise as we saw the profile of a handsome young woman in her late twenties. The resemblance to Renata was uncanny.

Giulia beamed at Renata. "I liked this game, but I have a headache and a migraine. May I retire to bed?"

Renata nodded, tears in her eyes. "Yes, of course," she replied. Renata stood and put her arms around Giulia, kissing her gently. "We don't have to pretend any longer, Renata, the game is over. Your father has been found, you will be reunited with him soon. But first, we need to revert to our original identities. You as Renata, and me, Giulia. I hope you understand?"

"Do you promise I will see my father? Are you sure it is safe?" asked Renata, her eyes wide and shining in childlike wonder.

"Yes, I swear it. Go to bed now, I will come and see you shortly."

And then, with a wide grin, the real Renata left the room. Giulia stared hard at Sherlock. "How long have you known?"

Sherlock sighed. "The moment I met you, it was evident you were trying to hide something or someone. At first, I thought you had taken a lover. But the feather Bauer and the red shoes Nene discovered under Renata's bed when we broke into your house a few days ago finally gave the game away."

"Yes, I'm sorry about that." I stared at her sheepishly. Giulia looked at us, astonished, as my husband continued his narrative.

"I first suspected your maid of being the doppelgänger at the insurance company. Still, after covertly questioning her when I posed as your gardener, I realised she lacked the mental capacity to commit such a heinous crime. There is almost a childlike endearing quality to her persona. She also spoke so affectionately of you, Signora Amato. I knew then she would be incapable of hurting anyone. During our many conversations at your house, she confessed how she liked to dress up in her late mother's clothes, wigs, and shoes, particularly those red heels. Then when she changed her apron in the kitchen, I noticed black hairs on her blouse. So it became obvious she wore a wig." Sherlock smiled gently at Giulia. "Now I have revealed all that transpired with your so-called husband and maid, will you now reveal to us your own secret?"

Giulia stared at Holmes incredulously. "All right." She nodded. "I fail to understand. If you already knew, why didn't you tell Inspector Romano?"

"Because first I want to hear your version of events."

Giulia sighed resignedly. "Very well, but before you judge

me, I would like to tell you the whole story."

Sherlock nodded, taking a seat across from Giulia. I almost laughed, observing Sophia and Robert's slack-jawed expressions as they stared at my husband in admiration.

"It was Renata's idea for me to impersonate her, not mine. Whatever you may think of me, I want that to be clear from the outset." She sighed. "On the day of the crash, there were five of us in the carriage returning from our holiday in Rome. Renata and I, my mother, and Renata's parents. One moment we sat there talking and laughing without a care in the world, the next a loud crash, and smoke billowed through the doors and windows. My mother ordered Renata and me to shelter in the luggage compartment, and then we got knocked out by the blast. When we came around, we found our parent's lifeless bodies. Someone shouted that help was on its way.

"Renata was inconsolable. Not only had she lost her beloved adoptive parents, who had worked tirelessly to keep her safe, but she was concerned she would be sent to the asylum without living relatives to protect her. She begged me to swap identities with her until she came of age and received her inheritance, so I reluctantly agreed. I couldn't bear the thought of anything happening to my friend. She was fundamental in the structure of my life. And, of course, with my beloved mother gone and no other 1relatives, I was in a similar position. We agreed we had lost so much, we couldn't lose each other. So we decided to swap clothes and identities. We had always looked alike. Even the domestic staff sometimes struggled to tell us apart. We were only indistinguishable by the birthmark that Renata later concealed with makeup. However, Renata was slightly taller and had smaller pupils. People often remarked about our resemblance and mistook us for sisters whenever we played together in the garden.

"The ambulance took us to the hospital after the accident to be checked over by the doctors. Due to her previous history, Renata underwent a mental health assessment. Of course, she passed with flying colours. The doctors were amazed by her progress. Because, of course, it was me, posing as her again. The lawyers allocated a small allowance but adequate for us to live comfortably. Renata insisted I continue my singing and piano lessons.

"When Renata came of age, I suggested we resume our normal identities, but she would not hear of it. You see, by then, she was becoming more dependent on me. Renata's behaviour can be challenging. Due to the traumatic brain injury she suffered as a child, she sometimes becomes aggressive and violent when she forgets to take her medication. But besides that, Renata is a kind, gentle, loving soul. She even developed a relationship with a young man, Tommaso, a coach driver she met at church. Thankfully, Renata assures me it's a platonic relationship. I have no idea what will happen if she expects more. Although I don't think she is ready for a full relationship, I would hate for any man to take advantage of her."

Giulia shook her head. "I would rather die than allow her to be sent away. And you are correct, Signor Sapori, Renata was always obsessed with her mother's shoes and clothes. In particular, those red heels. When Benedetta died, Renata wore them all the time. That was her way of keeping her mamma close to her. I remember one day, something I said unwittingly made Renata cry. And when I looked at her, it was as though her whole world had imploded. So if you allow, Signor Sapori, if Renata's father rejects her, and I pray to god that he doesn't, then I would like to spend the rest of my life making sure my friend is safe. If you report us to the authorities, then god knows what will become of us."

I stared at Giulia in admiration. This woman, whose marriage was in tatters, would sacrifice her life for her friend. Then my gaze diverted to my beloved Sophia, whose own marriage was hanging by a thread. False promises and empty words cuckolded my friends. And at that moment, I somehow knew Sophia and Robert would be successful in their marriage.

"There is one thing that puzzles me." I turned my gaze to Renata. "Why did you hire a private detective to try and find Renata's biological parents? Surely that was a risky strategy."

"Oh, yes," said Giulia. "Indeed it was. But I did it for two reasons. First, I was concerned about how Renata would manage if anything happened to me. Second, I felt I owed it to my friend. I was devastated when I discovered Renata's birth mother was dead and her father was incarcerated for murdering a child. How on earth could I tell her that? I instinctively knew she would not be able to handle the truth, so I informed Renata that the private detective had been unable to find her father and she accepted that. The night you told me that Lorenzo was pardoned, I was ecstatic. It was the happiest day of my life. My beloved husband was coming home from the hospital and Renata would, at last, be reunited with her biological father. I believed that he would understand once I explained everything to Luigi. After all, we both had lucrative careers, and my husband had his theatre company. We did not need any inheritance. I had no way of knowing that our marriage was a complete sham, and Luigi married me for the money — for Renata's legacy."

"Your so-called husband is a bigamist,' said Sherlock. The irony is that he married a woman who was concealing her identity. However, as far as my wife and I are concerned, your secret is safe forever. Unfortunately, I cannot speak for the Moons."

"No one will hear a word from my lips," said Sophia, speaking to Giulia." You have my word on that. Your narrative has humbled me deeply. I realise how lucky I am to be surrounded by my family and friends."

Sherlock nodded to Sophia. "Thank you," he said. "That is most gracious of you, given the circumstances." He then turned his attention back to Giulia. "I shall write to Lorenzo Rossi immediately and explain all that transpired. I'm sure he will understand when I explain the circumstances. He is a good man who deserves to be reconciled with his daughter." Sherlock smiled sympathetically at Giulia. "I am moved beyond measure by what you did to protect your friend. Your remarkable fortitude is a fine testament to you as a human being. But, at least this way, you will be free to continue your career. Although, you will, of course, need to change your name."

Giulia nodded. "Thank you. I hope we can all remain friends. That is, If you wish to be associated with a governess's daughter."

"Don't be silly," I said. "You will always be my friend. You are welcome at our house anytime."

"Likewise," said Sophia as she stood and hugged our friend.

We said our farewells, and Robert and Sophia dropped Sherlock and me off at our villa. I had never felt so relieved to come home. How I longed to see my children.

I was at breakfast the next day when Sophia unexpectedly joined me in the morning room, asking to speak to Sherlock.

I raised an eyebrow. "Is that such a good idea? Given your past altercations?"

Sophia shook her head, taking a sip from her coffee cup. "I never thought I would say this, but I must apologise to your husband."

"But why?" I quizzed.

"Because what Sherlock did last night, his courage and tenacity, the way he conducted himself to protect us, took my breath away. He was something to behold. And I realised then what you see in him. How you look at your husband with kindness and tenderness even though you are aware of all his foibles. And the fact that you see this, Nene, humbles me immensely. I have mocked your marriage so many times, and I am truly sorry for that. For it is you, my darling, amongst all of us, who is the lucky one."

I gestured to the garden. "He's out there, tending to his bees. But be careful, don't get too close to the hives."

My words fell on deaf ears as Sophia dashed into the garden. Half an hour later, Holmes and Sophia joined me to take coffee. Although they never discussed what happened during their conversation, nevertheless, the atmosphere between the two was congenial. Sherlock even cracked a joke. And as for me, I felt genuinely content that two of the people I cared for most in the world were now reconciled.

EPILOGUE

Milo Endrizzi passed away peacefully at the Policlinico hospital two days later. He never got to see his brother. Sherlock and I attended the funeral, a quiet, sombre affair, along with Milo's sister, Olivia, and the nurse who had looked after him. There was an incredible aura of tranquillity as the pallbearers lowered the coffin to the ground. The priest's last words ended in a haunting silence. There is an inevitability about death I had never witnessed so nobly as by Milo Endrizzi. I prayed he would find eternal rest and that god would have mercy on his soul.

Lorenzo and his daughter were finally reunited. He sold Milo's house and hotel and moved in with Renata—a little family who had suffered incredibly trying to heal themselves. Giulia bought an apartment in the old town, although she regularly met up with Renata and her father. She continued her career at La Scala under her birth name.

Luigi and Edoardo remained in jail, awaiting trial. Edoardo's sister was arrested for attempted fraud and for helping to pervert the course of justice. The Australian federal police finally caught up with Angelo Endrizzi, in New South Wales, and he was deported back to England, awaiting trial.

Some events in life have a sense of déjà vu—even when you've caught up in the midst of them, you somehow know the memories will stay with you forever.

Three days after Milo's funeral, we finally took our trip to Fiesole, where we were reunited with our beloved children and the Espiritos. Charlotte shrieked with delight upon seeing her father. Later that night, while Nicco and Charlotte slept in the farmhouse, Sherlock and I made ourselves comfortable on the porch that was so familiar. I asked my husband a question that had been on my mind for some time.

"I know that many of your clients have been women. But, tell me, I'm curious. Have you ever been tempted to stray? I have had a little wine, Sherlock, so I am calm. Please tell me the absolute truth, not what you think I want to hear."

My husband looked at me with a bemused expression. "No, of course not, why would I?" He paused for a moment. "I supposed there was that unfortunate incident with the maid in the Charles Augustus Milverton case."

"Sherlock, I did not believe you at the time, and I refuse to believe you now. If I did, that would mean you were engaged three times and married twice. Not bad for a misogynist who finds most women inscrutable."

He sighed. "We have been through this before. That was an unnecessary ploy to solve the case. I promised it would never happen again."

"I should think so, too."

"For god's sake, the woman was no more in love with me than I was with her. She used me to make the man she loved jealous — my hated rival — and it worked. As soon as I left, he appeared on the scene and took over, professing his undying love and they married soon after."

"But what if she had fallen hopelessly in love with you?"

"Apart from a chaste kiss, nothing physical developed between us. I would never have allowed that to happen. You knew from the outset that there were other women in my past. You were not the first, although you will undoubtedly be the last." He sighed. "You need to understand that I love you, and when I think of you, I realise how fortunate I am to have the wife and family I do. My worst fear is that I would ever do anything to jeopardise that. But when I met you, I

thought you were the most intelligent, exciting, and complicated woman I had ever met, and nothing you say or do can
ever change that."

"All right then." I nodded. "I believe you. Tell me, how
long do you deduce we'll be together? And please don't give
me a quantitative answer."

Sherlock smiled, his face lined with emotion as he stared
into my eyes. "Only for as long as I breathe."

A tear ran down my cheek as I looked around the humble
barn where our story began all those years ago, and I smiled,
for it was here that love started and would forever remain. "I
guess that will have to do." I sighed, slipping my hand into
his. "Come. I think I hear Violetta calling us for dinner."

The End

ABOUT THE AUTHOR

KD Sherrinford was born and raised in Preston, Lancashire, and now resides on The Fylde Coast with her husband John, and their four children. An avid reader from an early age, KD was fascinated by the stories of Sir Arthur Conan Doyle and Agatha Christie. She had read the entire Doyle Canon by the time she was 13. A talented pianist, KD played piano from age six. The music of some of her favourite composers, Beethoven, Schubert, Stephen Foster, and Richard Wagner, all strongly feature in her writing.

KD had a varied early career, working with racehorses, show jumpers, and racing greyhounds. She and her husband won the Blackpool Greyhound Derby in 1987 with Scottie. Then to mix things up, KD joined Countrywide, where she was employed for over 20 years and became a Fellow of The National Association of Estate Agents.

Retirement finally gave KD the opportunity to follow her dreams and start work on her first novel. She gained inspiration to write *Song for Someone* from her daughter Katie, after a visit to the Sherlock Holmes museum on Baker Street in 2019. It had always been a passion to write about Irene Adler, she is such an iconic character. The first two books in this thrilling series, *Song for Someone* and *Christmas at the Sapori's,* are available now at all major outlets.

If you enjoy KD's books, she would love you to post a review.

KD can be found on her author page: https://www.facebook.com/KDSherrinford/Author.co.uk and also on her

website: www.kdsherrinford.co.uk
To find out the latest, email kdsherrinford@gmail.com